Guinevere Forever

Book One

Lost Camelot Series

By M.L. Bullock

ISBN 9781973560906

And slowly answered Arthur from the barge:
"The old order changeth, yielding place to new,
And God fulfils himself in many ways,
Lest one good custom should corrupt the world.
Comfort thyself: what comfort is in me?
I have lived my life, and that which I have done
May He within himself make pure! but thou,
If thou shouldst never see my face again,
Pray for my soul. More things are wrought by prayer
Than this world dreams of. Wherefore, let thy voice
Rise like a fountain for me night and day.
For what are men better than sheep or goats
That nourish a blind life within the brain,
If, knowing God, they lift not hands of prayer
Both for themselves and those who call them friend?
For so the whole round earth is every way
Bound by gold chains about the feet of God.
But now farewell. I am going a long way
With these thou seëst—if indeed I go
(For all my mind is clouded with a doubt)—
To the island-valley of Avilion;
Where falls not hail, or rain, or any snow,
Nor ever wind blows loudly; but it lies
Deep-meadowed, happy, fair with orchard lawns
And bowery hollows crowned with summer sea,
Where I will heal me of my grievous wound."

Excerpt from *The Passing of Arthur*

Alfred Lord Tennyson, 1859-1885

Dedicated to all those that dream of
the kings and queens of old.

I dream too.

Chapter One—Guinevere

People say that when you are dead you do not know anything. They say that the soul ceases to exist, that you cannot feel or see beyond the blackness. But all those wise and learned men, the ones who claim they know what lies beyond death's mystical doorway, are wrong.

All of them.

I have been dead a long time, and I feel everything. I see everything and know far too much.

*

Five floors below me, a young woman with pink hair and a raspy voice wanted to die. She fantasized about it daily in graphic detail as she vacuumed the carpets, and her reasons were as endless as her nail polish collection. Louise was her name. Working with her was Richard, whose daydreams were different but just as hopeless. Richard pined for his neighbor, Brenda, while he waxed the hallway floors night after night. He wondered how he would ever pay his hospital bills and thought perhaps it would have been better to die an early death. Another man, Carlos, the night watchman, stole change from a nearby desk and planned to set the building on fire.

This I would never allow.

Of the three, Carlos interested me the most. But not so much that I would engage in conversation with him, unless I decided to kill him.

And this was now my kingdom. I was the Queen of Death. I secluded myself in my tower away from the living except to plunder their minds...and sometimes their blood. And when they called for death, even subconsciously, I was drawn to them. For *I was Death.*

Some would revel in such knowledge; I had known men and women who would have killed for such an advantage, but these pitiful mortals were not my enemies. I had only one enemy—and for the first time in a hundred years, she was close and I waited. Morgan delayed for reasons of her own. Perhaps she was hesitant to face me after nearly seven hundred years because she knew I would kill her...and not quickly.

For now, I closed my eyes and lingered in my kistvaen. Its stone walls kept me cool and protected from the sun's rays, which were not yet extinguished. The glass windows of my penthouse were covered with expensive blinds set to retract after sundown. The sunlight would not harm me as it once had, for I was much stronger now, yet it repulsed me and would swiftly sicken me. However, on clear nights after I fed I often watched the world below for hours; sometimes I counted stars and pondered the surface of the moon. The nighttime celestial lights were my constant companions. The apartment had high, spacious ceilings and fine wood floors. Although it had hardly any furniture, it met my needs and shielded me from humanity—and others of whom I became increasingly aware.

Like the one who drew near now.

Morgan!

With relentless determination I continued searching for the mind of my enemy, but she eluded me.

Perhaps I had only imagined Morgan nearby—so deeply did I long for Camelot these interminable days.

Yes, I dreamed of Camelot. And not the fabled city with golden spires atop rising towers, the stuff of fairy tales and legends. No, I dreamed of Camelot as she first began, an encampment of wood and earth and fire. A stronghold built on courage, strength, love and trust.

Until trust was broken.

I dreamed of the Camelot that Arthur and I built with our bare hands—with our own blood, sweat and tears. Yes, so many tears, yet so much hope. We poured our souls into that bit of land and saw miracles arise from the sowing. Oh yes, we saw wonders, but all of that was forgotten now, lost in the shadows of time that swallowed everything. Like whitened dandelions, blown away by the gentlest of breezes, so was our city gone forever.

But my long memory recalled the days before the burning and the terror that came by night. I felt warm sunshine without fear then and tasted golden apples and was surrounded by the laughter of children—and I rested in my love for Arthur. Yes, I could see him now. Alive and laughing at his many merlins—how he loved those birds, and how he laughed at everything. Arthur rose in my memory, and I pictured him standing tall against his enemies, unafraid to fight whoever or whatever stood in his way. All for the Greater Purpose, as he called it. Sometimes he even fought with me, but he always loved me and I him. We had been inseparable for a time, and then he was gone.

Gone too soon, my Summer King!

Arthur Pendragon was myth to most now, his vibrancy reduced to an elusive idea that the modern world could not seem to grasp. Fashionable depictions of him frustrated me, for they were as far removed from reality as I was from those Glorious Days. Even our children had been forgotten, their names lost to the world. Their mother emerged in modernity's new mythologies as a barren husk of a woman; a wanton whose womb suffered the wrath of God for her indiscretions, who bore no son, no daughter. It was a tawdry fantasy that they enjoyed.

Ah, let it be. Let us all be forgotten by the world, but I never shall forget them. I will always remember my children. Arthur, I cannot let you go, my love...

If I could have shed tears, I would have let them flow, but any relief through tears escaped me. My tears were stolen by Morgan's curse, gone with my humanity. Yet I daily sought Arthur in my dreams as relentlessly as old Pellinore sought his Questing Beast. Pushing against the Unseen Hand, I demanded entrance into the dream world, for at least I could still dream. I spoke my husband's name, as if it were a key to the Otherworld, but I did not find him. Nor did he respond as he had in the beginning. This was an exercise in futility. As the sun blazed outside and humanity toiled in the building beneath me, I hid in stillness and hoped for a glimpse of those long-gone days.

And then, just when I was about to give up hope, the dream-fog shifted and I was no longer seeking entrance into Camelot but standing on the hills of Avalon.

I did not want to be here.

It was cold, and the snowflakes fell quickly and heavily. Three queens stood with me as silent witnesses to the most horrible moment of my life, save one. The sickening sound of mortar slapping on stone, the screech of a watching owl made the moment genuine and also unbearable. I observed a nameless man seal the stone wall as it climbed higher, and I knew that wall would forever separate Arthur and me.

The Bear of Britain, Arthur Pendragon, was dead. Betrayed and murdered. And gone down with him into the grave was the dream of Camelot, the Bright and Shining City for which we had given everything. Our fair dream and our time in the Summerland had come to an end. And even though I had been forewarned of the danger to Camelot, I would never have imagined her speedy demise.

We, four of the six remaining queens of Britain, stood between the sacred torches, our cold breath creating swirls of fog around our faces. And through a veil of tears we said goodbye to my husband and our king. When the last stone was in place, I waited for some words of comfort. Some hope. But there were no arms to fall into as there once may have been, no consolation for me.

Nimue vanished first, doubtless anxious to return to her hunt for Merlin, her lover and sometimes teacher. At least she did not scold me or blame me for Arthur's death. Even she had given up hope for his healing in the end.

"The Beast's blade was poisoned, my queen. The wound inflicted by Mordred is of the kind that cannot be healed by my hand. If only Merlin were here..."

And where was the man who'd put Arthur on the throne? Merlin, you failed us—you failed Arthur! I sent men to seek him out, but time was not our ally. I pleaded with the Powers on High to spare Arthur, to take my life if required, but my prayers were not answered. Not in the way I expected.

My husband died that night, never opening his eyes to wish me farewell. He had not spoken to anyone at all except Galahad, who left immediately without offer of explanation. When I finally returned to Arthur's side, he was in his forever rest.

Vivian, Lady of the Lake and Queen of Avalon, broke the circle next. Her cold stare blasted the full measure of her hatred toward me. I could almost feel her loathing, like a wave from her precious lake slapping against my soul. For a moment, I saw that faraway look in her eye, the look she always wore when she was about to speak for her goddess, but she relented and said nothing. She spoke a few words to her manservant in her secret language, and I jutted out my chin in defiance. Her servant, a hulking figure of masculine strength, paused with his hand on his blade before obediently following the Lady. I had done the unthinkable—refused to relinquish Excalibur into her hands—and I knew I had not heard the last of her. She would no doubt take to swords over possession of the sacred blade, as was her right, but I could not part with it. How could I? It was the last bit of Arthur left, and his blood remained on the steel. The king's blood had been shed—it was precious to me.

The Lady of the Lake was wrong if she believed I kept Excalibur only for myself. What of Lochlon? Was not my son the rightful heir? Some would say yes; some would say no. But I knew the truth—he was Arthur's son! Since the nobles and knights had not yet rallied around Lochlon, I would keep the sword until they came to their senses. It may have been wiser to bury Excalibur with Arthur, but Nimue had interceded.

Kind, dreamy-eyed Nimue. "Morgan will seek the sword, and Vivian will not deny her," she had whispered to me. "She would wield it and rule on a throne of blood. Do not release Excalibur, Guinevere. Arthur left it in your care."

Nimue had been right. Morgan was not above disturbing Arthur's secret resting place to claim the sword, and she would have the power to break any prayer or spell of protection. In the end, I hid Excalibur until I could think what my next move should be.

Ah, Morgan...even in my dreams, I felt the weight of your betrayal.

The mason finished his work, bowed his head to me and trudged away through the snow to leave me alone with my husband's monument. But I was not alone. Queen Igraine remained too. Tall and slender, Igraine's faded blond hair hung about her like heavy ropes. Her skin was as soft and white as her hair. It was not hard to believe that her loveliness had once nearly wrecked the peace of Britain. Arthur's mother had been a great beauty in her day and a force to be reckoned with. She had been as her son was, vibrant and optimistic in all things.

Except her daughter, Morgan. She never showed that child any love. It was as if all her love had been spent on Uther and then Arthur. There had been none left for little Morgan of the Fairies. But I had loved Morgan once.

In my memory-dream, I reached for Igraine to say something that would ease her suffering, but she turned away coldly and left me standing on the white hillside alone. And I was truly alone. I had no allies. My daughter, Alwen, had been stolen the night her father was wounded; my son, Lochlon, fled Camelot for his life; and Arthur's knights were dead or had disappeared from our land, unwilling to stand against Mordred, the son of Morgan and Accolon. How the young dragon had roared, but he was gone now too. Arthur had pierced his heart on Camlann's bloody field.

I collapsed on my knees, uncaring that the snow was gathering around me. Let it freeze me! Let it pile against me! I moaned, the grief carrying me into unknown places.

"Arthur!" I yelled, anger welling up within me. "Arthur!" But there was no answer. I heard nothing but the whistling of the wind and the sound of leaves collapsing under the weight of the heavy snow.

For what felt like an eternity, I wept there...and then the dream folded in on itself as they always did when it was time for me to awaken.

I blinked open my eyes and knew that I was not alone. I sensed her presence. Then I saw her—my sister-in-law, a woman I once called my own sister. Morgan LeFay perched on a dusty table on the far side of the room. She did not move or appear alive at all. In fact, she looked much like a stone gargoyle, squatting low with her thin arms wrapped around her folded legs. If not for my vampire eyes, I might have overlooked her, but I saw her.

Now, we shall see how this goes.

I sprang out of the kistvaen, shoving the stone lid to the ground with all my might, and with a furious scream raced toward her.

Chapter Two—Guinevere

"After all this time, I will have your life," I promised Morgan, my hunger rising along with my rage. My breath came quick and ragged as my hands wrapped around her jeweled neck, but she laughed at me in a strangled voice. Then her hands were on me and she swung me around, pinning me against the plain plaster wall and creating puffs of dust.

"Come now, let's be friends, sister-in-law. I have so much to tell you."

That proposal only infuriated me more. I pushed off the ground with my legs and lifted her off the floor, carrying her with me to the top of the high ceiling. I expected her to scream, to beg for her life, but she did none of those things and did not stop laughing. Baring my fangs, I lunged for her neck, but Morgan did not hesitate. She did not tremble or shake or beg for mercy. Something had to be amiss. And then she stopped laughing; her dark eyes pierced mine, and I shuddered at the pure hatred I saw in them.

"Kill me, and any chance of saving your miserable life—or Arthur's—dies with me." I did not drop her, although I wanted to more than anything. What a pleasure it would have been to see her fall and break into pieces! But she was strong and as determined as ever. *What kind of creature was Morgan now?* She was not of my kind but something else. Something I did not understand. The scent of musty leaves, forgotten herbs and a hint of rain permeated her skin.

"Empty words, Morgan."

"Are they? You would have Arthur's blood on your hands?"

"Arthur is dead. They are all dead—I am too!"

"You *are* stupid, aren't you? You know that some souls never die. Arthur is alive, Undead Queen, and he is not the only one. Another lives still—or do you at last care nothing for Lancelot? Have you finally purged your heart?"

Hearing their names spoken aloud surprised me, and my blood-hungry excitement waned for a few seconds as I pondered her words. After all this time, I knew that Morgan would not speak an idle word to me. If she came at me with threats, she always followed them up with the promised deed. Just like when she promised to destroy me, to make me suffer.

I refused to release her, and we locked eyes. "I am already dead, as you well know, and so are Arthur and Lancelot. You brought death to me. Perhaps it is time that I bring you under his shadowy wing. I have grown strong these many years, sister."

Then she vanished, and I was left clutching the air. I immediately descended and watched as the thin brunette reappeared on the other side of the room. "Ah, not as strong as I, again."

A snarl escaped my lips, and I sailed toward her. "Strong enough," I warned her, but she disappeared again. I screamed at the air around me, "Why are you here, Morgan? Have you come to gloat or merely to admire your creation?"

Morgan reappeared as if nothing had happened between us. She straightened her gown; she had been so meticulous a dresser when we were all young and alive. She did not meet my eyes, but her words conveyed her serious intent. "I want what belongs to me, Undead Queen. I want what is mine. Give me Excalibur, and I will let you die as a mortal. I think that is more than merciful considering your many crimes."

I sneered, "Merciful? When have you ever been merciful? And what crimes are you speaking of, Morgan? It is you who betrayed the king, you who stirred the pot and planted hatred in Mordred's heart." I paused and added, "Perhaps we should ask Accolon about your mercy."

"You dare speak his name," she said in a low tone. "The only man in all of Camelot that you could not seduce?" Her hand slammed the table, and I heard the wood crack under the force of it. "Give me the sword, Guinevere. It does not belong to you and never has. You may have lain with a Pendragon, but that does not make you one."

I did not take the bait. "Camelot is lost. You saw to that. The time of the Pendragons is over, Morgan. You cannot wield the sword, and I will not release it."

Her eyes glittered with that old familiar lust. So she had not changed. Had I expected that she would?

"Excalibur is mine to do with what I will. Give the sword to me, and I swear I will let you go. But if you refuse me, you will die...once and for all."

"You think I fear death? He is a familiar friend, sister. I have delivered many souls into his hands. He would welcome me with open arms, I think. Thanks to you."

Morgan hovered near the table again and watched my every move. I paced the floor, unsure whether to kill her or listen to her further. My red hair was a wild mess, my clothes were little more than rags, and I couldn't remember the last time I bathed. It had seemed such a meaningless human thing to do. I regretted that now.

"Maybe so, but you would not wish the same fate for Arthur...or Lancelot. Or do you no longer care for either of them?" My hand wrapped around a pewter statue of a stag, an old treasure that I kept for some sentimental reason. What could she mean? With Morgan, the truth was always hidden.

"You speak to hear yourself talk, Morgan." Even as I said this, dread crept up my spine.

"Do you remember that night, my queen? I imagine you must. How desperate you were to die. That was your sin, Guinevere. You thought you could escape the consequences of your actions; you sought the path of least resistance. If you had not put your lips on the vial, if you had not taken a sip, you would not be what you are now. You did this by your own hand! I did nothing."

"I never wanted to become a monster. Your trickery did this. You sent the girl; I know that now. I sought only to die, not to become this! Say what you have to say—speak plainly!"

Suddenly, a clock appeared on the table beside Morgan. It was not a modern clock but an hourglass full of red sand. Morgan turned the hourglass upside down and the sand began to fill the bottom half. "Tick, tock, tick, tock. You see this, my Undead Queen? The sands represent the seconds of your life, and not your life alone. When these sands disappear, when they are all poured out, the curse will end. It was a strong curse, as far as curses go, don't you think? Seven hundred years is impressive; I am sure even Merlin would agree with me." I purposefully revealed no emotion when she mentioned his name, and she continued, "Sadly, all good things must come to an end. I stretched it as long as I could, and I hope you have enjoyed your time, but now you must go down into the darkness forever. Unless you are willing to give me Excalibur."

"You know I am not. And I never will!"

Her face twisted into a picture of spite. "Then your fate and the fates of your lovers are sealed!" She banged her fists on the table, breaking it now, and stood in front of me. "For you see, this curse touched not only you but Arthur and Lancelot as well. I did not lie to you, Guinevere. While you have spent your time in darkness, they have come again and again into this world and you never knew them. But now they will die the final death and go wherever it is they will go. As for you, Undead Queen," she said as she grinned and her overly large eyes widened with excitement, "you will disappear into the darkness, never to be remembered again by any of those you love. You will be forgotten by all. And if someone does remember your name, they will think it a curse and not a blessing."

"You have already seen to that," I growled as she gave me a mock curtsy. She waited to hear my answer. What should I say? I knew Morgan was not here for her mere amusement. She had a plot in mind. "Morgan, stop this madness! All we have fought for, all we have fought over, has ended. Your brother and Camelot are gone, and they will never rise again. The time for such things is over. The world is a different place."

Like a wild cat, Morgan let out a scream that stunned me. She moved as fast as one too. She now stood on top of my tomb, and she'd moved faster than I could think. "Do you think I care anything for Camelot? Do you think I care about the passing of knights and Round Tables? You know what I want. Give me Excalibur! It is within my power to let you die in whatever way you choose. And as a kindness, I will not harm Arthur or Lancelot du Lac."

Maybe she was telling the truth. I had noticed that my hunger had faded recently. Could it be a sign that the curse's magic waned?

What should I do, Arthur?

Long ago, Arthur had been everything to Morgan; she had been his greatest champion until Lancelot arrived. Perhaps that was her true reason for hating the knight so—her unrequited love. I had come to believe that had been the reason she spread those lies about Lancelot and me, for I know she was the one who sowed those seeds of rumors.

In the beginning. Before they were true.

"I know where he is, Guinevere. I know where Arthur is." She flashed a disturbingly sweet smile. "He is handsome, as handsome as he was before. He looks much the same, in fact." I stared at her as she giggled like a maid gossiping over a new suitor. "This new Arthur, he could rule Camelot if he had the sword."

My heart sank at hearing her talk so freely of Arthur. "I am not giving you the sword, Morgan. For no price would I give you Excalibur, and I would never believe you desired it for Arthur."

She tapped her black painted fingernail on her narrow chin. "I am beginning to think you do not have the sword at all, Guinevere. I think you lost it, or you gave it to that buffoon conjuror, Merlin. You are lying to me, Undead Queen. You do not know where the sword is—I can see the truth just there behind those dark eyes." As she accused me, I began to read her mind. But as soon as I walked into the room of her memories, she slammed the door on me. She wagged her finger at me and said, "No, no, no. That's cheating."

"I will not give you the sword, and that is my final answer. Leave us alone, Morgan, or you will pay!"

Then I felt her mental probing, and I shut the door on her too.

"Clever queen...so you have learned a few things. But it won't do you any good. I know you, Guinevere, like I know my own self. You are the other side of me, I think," she said in her childlike dreamy voice. Then her fury came back. "I will find the sword, for it will also be close to its master." Morgan's face brightened at her own revelation. "Yes! Excalibur draws close to the Pendragon! It will find him. Never mind...I do not need you after all." She walked toward the locked door. "I think I shall go pay my brother a visit. I doubt he will remember me, not at first, but then again maybe he will. And perhaps he will remember you and your Great Betrayal. I wonder, will the Bear of Britain have the heart to forgive you, Undead Queen? I am happy that I do not require your help after all; that is a great comfort to me." With that, she waved her hand and the door opened. She walked out and slammed it behind her, again without touching it.

My mind reeled with what I had just learned. First, it was possible to read Morgan's mind, yet in doing so, I left my own mind open for her to plunder at will. Second, she did not know that I *had* seen Arthur many times, in many incarnations, over the years. Yes, I had managed to keep that to myself. It had been only in the past hundred years or so that I stopped seeking him out. I had to put an end to torturing myself. Had I made a mistake? It would seem so—now Morgan had the advantage over me. She would find Arthur, hold him until the sword found him, and then kill him as she had always planned. This time, she would not have Accolon around to do her dirty work.

No, Morgan would do her own blood work. For some reason, I did not think that would be a problem for her. There was nothing human left in Morgan. Like me, she was a creature through and through.

And she was coming for Arthur.

Chapter Three—Guinevere

I headed to the Saint James Museum, an odd, out-of-the-way facility that had been the location for town hangings in the thirteenth century. Too much blood had been shed in the village of Saint James; it had never been a happy place. But now, it was a place where I sometimes sought the company of others—from a safe distance, of course—and I appreciated the exhibits here, which were often unseen by the masses. This I also appreciated. I continued to be drawn to the old paintings and various artifacts that occasionally made their way to the dusty halls of the three-story building. I was like one of these relics, very old and largely forgotten. But that was a good thing for a vampire, wasn't it?

I thought again of the original Saint James village as I made the short trip out of the Wells building and to the museum. The Warwick family, its founders, had been a suspicious lot, but they proved themselves noble and true to the Pendragon right up until the end. During the beginning of my time as Queen of Camelot, this area served as a training field, a field for jousting and weapons practice, and many died here. I always hated watching the jousting tournaments and never understood why men would risk their health and limbs just to unseat another man from his horse. What glory was there in that?

"There is no substitute for readiness," Arthur would remind me. "The warriors of Camelot cannot fall idle, Guinevere." Strange that I would remember such a thing tonight of all nights.

What do I do now, Arthur? I have not readied myself at all. Never would I have believed I would need to do so. How do I protect you?

I stepped inside the building unworried that anyone would notice me. Hardly anyone visited this museum, especially at night. But I remembered to keep my face hidden with a scarf, as my paleness surprised people sometimes, especially when I had not taken blood. Tonight, my hunger did not compare to my worry over Arthur. What was I going to do? Risk revealing my husband to the enemy of his soul or stay away and hope for the best? I practically flew up the metal stairs and walked so lightly I hardly made a sound. I paused on the landing to watch a professor, a man named John Faraday, who worked late here nearly every night. This evening, he obsessed over a cache of coins given to him by a curious schoolteacher who had discovered them in an old wooden box buried in her garden. Faraday never noticed me. His mind was so easy to read, but I liked that about him. He was an innocent, one of the few left in this world. Obsessed with the past, Faraday believed he had been born in the wrong time. And maybe he had been. Through the ages, my views on such things had changed dramatically.

I walked past his doorway and hovered outside a small room used for housing a rarely visited exhibit. The lights in the room were out, save one dim lamp. It was sometimes left on for whatever reason; it was on now, yet the door was closed and locked. That was a new development, but it wouldn't deter me. I was strong. I gripped the handle, twisted it and opened the door as if it had never been locked. The sparse room was bathed in cold purple light that filtered in through high windows. A seven-foot statue stood in the middle of the space, leaving room for only one bench used for viewing. To my surprise, the statue room had another visitor. I paused in the doorway and considered the implications—what human would sit in a room with a statue behind a locked door? Yes, she was definitely human of some sort. I could smell her blood and hear her heart racing. Whoever she was, she believed she had a reason to be here. And she seemed to be expecting me.

I stepped back, saddened that I would not be able to spend time alone with the statue that so reminded me of my lost love, Lancelot. I came here from time to time and consulted him in all manner of things. Not that statues could speak, and I did not believe that it was Lancelot in stone, but being here comforted me.

"No, wait. You do not have to leave. I will not be here long," a soft, feminine voice called to me.

I answered tentatively, "I did not mean to interfere." *Was this friend or foe?*

"Come inside. Come closer."

I closed the wooden door and stood by it, unwilling to look up into Lancelot's face in the presence of another. She did not seem to notice, for her eyes never left him.

"This plaque says he is Odo, Duke of Kent, but that is a mistake, isn't it? I have known many men of Kent and none as handsome as this one; his face is...exceptional. Such honesty and valor displayed in every feature. Don't you think he has a handsome face?" The girl in the blue cloak did not turn her attention from the statue, and her face was obscured by a hood. I felt a sting of jealousy, but for what? And for whom? Why should I feel jealous?

The girl pushed back her soft blue hood, which suddenly seemed quite familiar to me, and stared up at me from her spot on the bench. My heart could not believe what my mind told me. For hundreds of years I had seen familiar faces in crowds and heard voices I knew from my own time, and now I was looking into the face of someone who should not be here. The voice fit the face, and the face matched the one in my memory down to the last detail.

This was Elaine, the daughter of King Pellinore, my former lady-in-waiting and the wife of Lancelot. She smiled up at me, the dimples in the corners of her mouth on full display.

"Yes, quite handsome," I answered quietly. Elaine touched the statue's hand, and I noticed her clothing. This was not modern attire; she wore a gown of the softest blue with bell sleeves that laced at the shoulders. There were faded ribbons at her bosom and in her pale hair, which was woven into a small braid that encircled her head. In all these years, I had seen ghosts on rare occasions. If she was a ghost, she would be an unusual one because I swore

I could hear her heartbeat and smell her blood. And if she was Elaine, why would she come here now?

"A face to die for, wouldn't you say?" the woman with Elaine's face asked without a trace of a smile. Suddenly, she was all seriousness but so far not threatening. Protective, but not threatening...so like Lady Elaine.

"Who are you?" I asked, still unsure who stood before me.

"You do not know me, my queen? That is disappointing after all we went through together." Her voice saddened, and her eyes turned back to gaze upon Lancelot's face. "After all we fought for. After all we shared."

"Elaine," I said. It wasn't a question. It was certainly her, or some form of her.

"Why have you come here?" she asked accusingly. "You come too often."

"You have seen me here before? Why have you not come to me? He is not here, Elaine." That old feeling of protection welled up within me. Elaine had always been a fragile creature, one we all wanted to protect. We had been friends once.

"Yet, you are here. I ask you again, why have you come, Queen Guinevere?"

"Because visiting him...visiting here gives me strength. I have to...do something," I confessed with a truthfulness that startled me.

“Still leaning on Lancelot for strength,” she said with a frown.

My eyes focused as her image faded slightly. Elaine was losing strength. The heartbeat sound had stopped—I now realized it was a trick of hers—and I could no longer smell blood. There was no one living in this room. The dead Elaine wasn’t nearly as strong as I, but I could not find it in my heart to treat her unkindly. Not after all this time. “I never meant to hurt you, Elaine. You were my friend.”

Her image brightened slightly, but she did not fully materialize. She remained by Lancelot, her hand on his. “Why are you here?”

“I am here for Arthur. Morgan has returned. She wants Excalibur in exchange for Arthur’s safety...and, she says, Lancelot’s.” There was no sense in mincing words with Elaine. She was beyond my help now, and if she could help me, I would not refuse it.

Elaine’s round face darkened slightly. “There are no answers here, Queen Guinevere. Only emptiness. But as you say, Lancelot is not here. Go to Arthur now. It is him you must shield from Morgan’s plot.”

Feeling desperate and strangely excited at speaking to someone who knew me, the real me, the words gushed forth. “I cannot right the wrongs of the past, Elaine, but I cannot allow harm to come to Arthur or Lancelot. Not after all this time. I’m not sure what I should do.”

Elaine again stared at Lancelot. Her absolute devotion to him, even after all this time, surprised me. "If you have come to inquire of Lancelot, you already know his answer. Lancelot would protect Arthur with his heart, his body and his blood; he would always protect his king. He was the bravest, the strongest and the most loyal of all the king's knights. He would stay with Arthur—no matter what it cost him. You needn't linger here to ponder what you already know, Queen Guinevere. My husband gave his life for Camelot and Arthur...and you. Go now and leave us be. You have no right to ask anything else of us." In a flash of dim light, Elaine vanished, but I sensed her eyes watching me. Her presence hovered, still not threatening but protective of her husband.

"Elaine..." I pleaded with her, but then I changed my mind. What would that accomplish? She was but a ghost, perhaps even a figment of my own guilt and imagination. Lancelot was not here; he could not be consulted. I had no reason to believe he had not returned as Arthur had, but I had never seen him despite my attempts to find him...and much to my dismay. I would never have believed in such things when I was alive. Father Patrick would certainly never have instructed us in these matters, but now here I was still alive while he was ashes in the grave. *Better than to be like me. Eternally dead.* It was time to leave. Coming here had been a sentimental, foolish mistake. And I was wasting time.

The room was quiet now, but a sound from outside the door caught my attention. A stirring of the air, as if someone had opened a very large window. Elaine was right; I had no time for languishing here with this statue—Lancelot was indeed gone. And I needed to go now, but where? Would I really risk contacting Arthur? What good was a disgraced queen with no allies? What if Morgan was waiting for me to reach out to him? Moving silently through the museum, I sailed toward the exit. Not the front door this time but the side entrance that led out to the alleyway. Faraday still pondered over his coins, but he would be leaving soon. I resisted the urge to pay him a visit. Such a gentle soul did not deserve to die at my hands.

When I fed next, it would be vicious and bloody. Besides, I had another in mind. No, I would leave John Faraday as I found him, alive and pining for the past. I needed to prepare for my inevitable journey.

Just then, I spotted the sword of Britain on full display. Although coupled with other historic reproductions and incorrectly labeled as a sword of undetermined ownership, I knew it as well as I knew one of my own children. *Excalibur!*

Reaching for it, I touched the hilt. It wasn't housed in glass as I expected it would be. It was in full view, and presumably anyone could touch it as I did now. When I put my hand on the weapon, I immediately knew it was not the true sword. It held no life, no magic. What I held in my hand was a fantastic reproduction; the weight was wrong, the craftsmanship shoddy upon closer inspection and the renowned energy of the magical sword certainly absent. I put it back.

Then I realized the truth.

If this was a reproduction, then someone had seen the original. No one could have imagined so precise a copy without having laid eyes upon Excalibur. Plainly scripted in the runes of Avalon was Arthur's motto on the blade. I could no longer delay my duty. Morgan had been wrong about Excalibur and me. I remembered full well where the sword lay hidden, and I knew exactly where I placed it.

But what if her theory about Excalibur and Arthur was correct? What if the sword was trying to find its way back to him? It was not yet in her possession, but she would find a way—Morgan was a resourceful woman. There was only one way to find out, and if I did this, I would not be able to turn back. I would have to see it through and abandon my resting place...and hope that I could find something suitable to replace it.

Hunger cramped my stomach, I felt cold and tired, as I always did when I failed to take life. With the last of my strength, I slipped out of the museum and into the smelly streets of Old Thistledown.

Hungry or not, I needed to see Excalibur with my own eyes. And ready or not, eventually I would have to find Arthur. I had to protect him, serve him, as I always had. Just as Lancelot always had.

No matter what it cost me.

Chapter Four—Luke Ryan

The ground shook, and for one horrible moment I imagined the worst. The screams echoing from the chamber confirmed that I wasn't just imagining the worst—it had probably happened. One of my crew was in danger—Markie, Wheeler's kid, a newbie but a valuable member of our tight-knit team. Markie was full of spit and vinegar, as my old man would say, always anxious to prove himself to the older, more experienced miners. Especially his father. But I'd made the wrong decision, buckled under pressure and allowed Markie the chance to prove his toughness. The kid had no business handling the dud—that had been my task. I'd been the one to send him in, too. We should have told McAllister to screw off; we should have waited for the robot. It would have taken a day to get here, and the company would have lost money, but I didn't give a damn about that. Nothing was more important to me than my guys. They were my family.

Barreling past Buddy and Pint, I ran pell-mell through the cloud of smoke that billowed from the mine's portal. *What the hell had I been thinking?* "Markie!" I yelled as I ignored Buddy's warning and ran to the end of the passage, taking a left at the fork. Another scream issued from somewhere deeper in the mine, which got my adrenaline and legs pumping faster. I covered my mouth with a rag from my pocket as thick dust and heat assaulted my throat. I sweated as I ran—I had to be getting close to the newbie now, but I couldn't see a damn thing. I came to an obstruction that I couldn't navigate, a rock pile. Make that multiple rock piles. They littered the cave floor so it looked like I was walking on a strange, Martian landscape. Or in Dante's inferno. "Mark!" I yelled, tucking the rag in my back pocket and coughing my brains out.

A moan echoed through the chamber, and I raced toward the sound. Markie Wheeler was sprawled out in front of me, a cascade of rocks across his back and legs. I knelt down beside him, radioed back for more helping hands and began digging my guy out.

"Talk to me, kid. Can you hear me? Talk to me, Markie!"

He coughed and moaned and said, "I would if you'd shut up...sir."

I couldn't help but grin at hearing his attitude. "That's great, Markie. Keep it up. Don't move, though. We've got a medic right outside; we'll get you out." And then the cave shook. The Cavanaugh Mine threatened to seal us both in, putting an end to any further gold extraction—or human extraction, for that matter.

"I'm sorry, boss. The thing just blew before I could get to it." He was crying now, his courage gone, and I wanted to cry along with him.

"Cut that bull out. You don't have any reason to apologize, Markie. It should have been me in here, not you."

I could hear voices approaching us from the entrance. It was Wheeler, Pint and Buddy, along with the rest of the guys who were brave enough to enter this death trap. They fearlessly faced the danger to rescue their brother...or in Wheeler's case, his son. Although they were father and son, Norman Wheeler and Markie looked nothing alike. Wheeler was short and bald with serious black eyebrows that were easily his most notable feature. Markie was as light as his father was dark, with pale skin, white-blond hair and light blue eyes. He was an oddity, or so I'd thought when I first met him. He looked like a creature you might expect to find living in a cave that had never seen the light of day. But Markie took the ribbing about his looks good-naturedly, and he worked hard. And today when the dynamite didn't explode, he demanded the opportunity to fix the problem. The kid had the chops to replace the wick and reset the charge, but something had gone horribly wrong.

As I moved the rocks from his body, I could plainly see that Markie was seriously hurt. He looked like someone who'd been stoned by an angry mob of giants. I was sure parts of him were crushed; he was bleeding at his temple and from his nose. Some of his fingers were mangled, and he had the wide-eyed look of someone in shock.

"Son, speak to me," Wheeler said as he got down beside Markie. I called the medics in, and we set about securing the room as best we could so the team could evacuate the kid safely. After we had worked for what seemed like an eternity, the rescue team was finally carrying Markie out.

As I walked beside him and his father, I knew I had made a serious mistake. “Wheeler, I am so sorry. I truly am.”

“No sense in being sorry. This is the way he wanted it. You know Markie; he had to prove to everyone that he was a true-blue miner.”

“He’s done that. He’s true blue to the bone. Like his old man.”

The emergency workers would not allow me to ride with the guys to the hospital; Wheeler would ride inside. And although the rest of the crew assured me I had done nothing wrong, I knew the truth. I shouldn’t have let Markie go in, but I did. And now I would have to live with that for the rest of my life. *Come on, kid. You have to make it!*

“Heavy is the head that wears the crown,” Buddy said as we watched the truck leave, the red lights flashing and siren screaming. That seemed an odd thing to say to me right now.

“What?”

“It’s not important. Come on. Let’s go to the Questing Beast. They have a special on burgers and beers tonight. Wheeler will call us when he learns something.”

“I’m not hungry. Besides, I think I need to go to the hospital. I need to be there for Markie.”

"Leave it be. Leave it be, Ryan. Let Markie and Wheeler have their time together. You go see him tomorrow."

You mean whatever time they have together. What if there is no tomorrow for Markie?

Of course, I kept that thought to myself. I climbed in Buddy's van, and we headed to the local pub, a place called the Questing Beast Tavern. As we pulled up, I could see some of my guys had already arrived. With glum greetings, they set about drinking the day's horrible events away, and I joined them at the bar. I always sat near the door, and tonight I could hear the wooden sign swing in the breeze. For the life of me, I couldn't figure out why I liked sitting in this spot so much. We sat quietly, none of us talking much as we waited for a call from Wheeler. And while we waited, we drank. I passed on the burgers but drank until I was bleary-eyed. My heart broke for Markie, and I couldn't help but replay the day's events again in my mind. I recalled every detail of this morning, of drilling the hole, packing the dynamite, running the lines. We had followed every procedure; we had done everything right, and it still hadn't mattered. Misfires happened from time to time, but I should never have sent a greenhorn into the mine—that should always be my job. If anyone was going to die for the Cavanaugh Mining Company, it should have been me.

"Accidents happen, Ryan. Beating yourself up over it isn't doing that young man any good. What could you have done to prevent it? See the future?" As always, Buddy Moran stood by me in word and deed, but even he hadn't liked the idea of Markie going in.

"You knew, I think. You told me not to send him."

Buddy shook his head as if he disagreed with my memory. "You can't change the past, my friend. I just hope..."

"Stop right there. Don't say out loud what you don't want to see happen." We didn't talk much after that. It was so quiet that we could hear the clock tick on the wall. Murray continued to pull beers from the draught. I don't think anyone ordered food.

No one called to give us any news, and I feared the worst with every passing minute. How many people could survive an explosion like that? None that I'd ever heard of. It would take nothing short of a miracle for Markie to survive the crushing and pounding of a half-ton of stones. And where had Buddy gone to? He was just here beside me at the bar, and now the old man was gone.

"Buddy?" I called toward the half-open door of the only restroom. There was no light on inside the dank bathroom, and he didn't answer me. *That's great. He was my ride.*

I glanced up at the clock; it was half past nine. And then I remembered Michelle. Damn! I had a date tonight...it was our one-year anniversary, and I'd forgotten all about it. Some part of me wanted to call her and explain, but I knew she wouldn't understand. Besides, I couldn't for the life of me remember when I last saw my phone today, and the phone on the wall demanded a pocket full of change that I didn't have. A perfumed stirring of air beside me drew my attention away from the muted television. Every eye in the room was on the exotic-looking woman who made herself at home beside me.

"Mister Ryan. Just the man I was looking for."

"Do I know you, lady?"

With a mysterious smile, she answered, "I don't know. Do you?"

How to answer that? I couldn't imagine what she wanted, but I knew one thing for sure—she was going to be trouble. Pretty faces like hers always came with a big helping of that, and I had no mind for games.

"McAllister send you?"

"No, Mr. Ryan. Mr. McAllister did not send me."

"Lawyer, then?"

She laughed, but it didn't sound genuine. No, this woman had an agenda. "Short and sweet. That's how you like it, isn't it? I like that." She nodded once and offered me her hand. I shook it, but only so I could spur this conversation along.

She dropped my hand and gave me a soul-piercing look. "Let's try this again. Are you Luke Ryan?"

Chapter Five—Morgan LeFay

The man I once called brother looked at me; his empty expression humored me no end, but laughing in his face would not help my cause. Here was the Bear of Britain, the son of the Dragon, drowning himself in stale beer surrounded by human fools and the common trappings of modern life. Gone were his red banners embroidered with gold dragons. His great hall had fallen to the ground long ago, the timbers rotten, and even the mighty stones that supported the weight of the keep had broken. I wished he could see it. Such a sight would break his heart if I could trigger his past life memory. And I wanted him to feel broken as I felt broken. I wanted him to know the pain of losing everything for a second time.

"My, how the mighty have fallen!" I murmured.

"What?"

"Nothing. Just an unimportant observation, Mr. Ryan. Bartender, may I have something to drink? A whiskey, please? No ice." Within seconds, a stringy-haired man set an amber-colored drink in front of me. "My name is Morrigan, Lucy Morrigan. I am here with a proposal for you, Mr. Ryan."

He gave me a perturbed frown and said, "I'll be honest, Lucy. I'm not looking for company—or any other type of proposal. So if you don't mind..."

So like Arthur to think every woman in the world wanted him. Even his own sister. Strange...I had imagined that I would relish this introduction much more than I actually was. All I felt at the moment was frustration. How could he so easily forget me? Forget who he was? I never could. Not in a hundred lifetimes. Didn't that prove my claim that I should have the sword—that I was the true Pendragon? My allies agreed with me, and they were gathering closer. Soon they would be strong enough to slip through the veil and into this world.

And then what fun we would have!

"There is a rumor that you may soon need a job, Luke. May I call you Luke, or do you prefer Mr. Ryan?"

His face crumpled, and he turned away from me and stared at the television while he sipped his beer. *Oh my, how easily I struck at your pride, brother. At least that has not changed.* "Who told you I needed a job?"

"It stands to reason, doesn't it, Mr. Ryan? You had a misfire today, and a sacrifice was made. Now, I'm not assigning blame. I understand these things, Luke. Some people are expendable, but the Cavanaugh Mining Company understands that too. And they aren't going to support you if the tide turns against you. Cavanaugh will always put their best interests first. That's the law of the corporate jungle, Mr. Ryan."

"I didn't sacrifice anyone. It was an accident. And if I'm such a screw-up, why are you here? If you think I'm damaged goods, if I'm willing to sacrifice someone to get the job done, why would your company want me? Seems kind of counterintuitive for someone who knows the law of the corporate jungle." He drained the remainder of the beer from his glass and raised it for a refill. Arthur cut his hazel eyes at me and clenched his jaw. How alike he was to the man I knew as king! Oh yes, this would be delightful. I could not wait to tell him how much I enjoyed spending time with Alwen before she died. Poor fool of a girl. Loyal until the end, even when her mother's crimes were laid before her.

"I didn't say you purposefully put anyone in harm's way, Mr. Ryan. My apologies. I can see that you are the kind of man who feels responsible for his crew. To be honest with you, that's one of the reasons why the company I represent, Malvin Enterprises," I said with another smile as if my lie were the truth, "would like to hire you. We have a silver mine, small but incredibly lucrative with a newly discovered vein. This is a once-in-a-lifetime deal, Luke."

"Silver? How come this is the first I've heard of it? And I've never heard of Malvin Enterprises." As he appraised me, I could see he didn't quite believe me. Shrewd man, less trusting now. as to be expected.

"Nevertheless, I was sent to meet with you, and here I am. I've got a huge vein of silver to move, Mr. Ryan, but if you're not interested, I understand." I dug in my jacket pocket and removed a business card. Placing it in front of him, I swallowed the whiskey. It burned my throat, but I didn't flinch. The warmth it created excited me. I felt my cheeks warm and wondered if it looked like I was blushing.

I hoped so, as that would help my attempt at appearing human. How long had it been since I'd had a good blush? Blushing exuded weakness, and I was nothing if not strong. I'd had to be strong and demanding, or else I would have been left behind. Once I had been loved, even celebrated, but then Arthur had come along. The young Dragon had robbed me of my parents' love...and my birthright. Who would ever believe that Lochlon was the son of Arthur? He looked nothing like him, and that fact was the object of much gossip at court. Lochlon was dark, and Arthur was light. And Guinevere... Well, she had never been true to my brother, and he had been a fool to think otherwise. Mordred, my own son, Lancelot's son—the true blood of the Pendragon—should have been presented the sword. They should've bent the knee to him while they had a chance.

Arthur... We could have ruled as one, my brother. If only you would've put her away. If only you would've put Britain first. But here we are now. And I will have Excalibur!

"Hello? Miss Morrigan?"

"Oh, sorry. Daydreaming. It is well past my bedtime, Mr. Ryan. What did you say?"

"I just told you I don't need a job." He eyeballed me as if I were a blabbering fool. My patience was wearing thin. And time truly was of the essence; that part had not been a lie. I could feel the strength of my curse waning. Whatever was to be done had to be done now.

"And I told you that I hear things, Luke. You have the reputation of being a risk-taker. I like that characteristic in a leader, and so does the interest I represent. To put it bluntly, Luke Ryan, I want you."

He sat up stiffly in his seat and stared at me, his eyes red from beer. "Who did you say you were again?"

Masking my rage with a blank smile, I repeated myself as if I were speaking to a small child who had forgotten his lines at a school play. "Lucy Morrigan. I represent Malvin Enterprises. Keep my card, Mr. Ryan. You might need it sooner than you think." His jaw clenched again, but he didn't argue with me. I loved these human moments. I had so few of them nowadays. Without waiting for an answer or any further arguments, I left my card in front of him and walked out of the bar. I felt Arthur's eyes on me as I made my way out the door, and I couldn't help but smile. I would hear from him soon enough.

Unfortunately, the young man had not died as I had planned, but surely there would be enough damage to the mine that things would go the way I wanted. Yes, my friend would make that happen. I smiled up at the moon as if it were in on my plans. Yes, that had gone well, even if it was a subtler approach than I would have used in years gone by. A less patient version of me would have gone into the Questing Beast with guns blazing, like a villain in an Old West film. I liked the picture shows, and tales of the American West were my favorite. Probably because I had such an affinity for that time period. So much freedom, so little law. Yes, those had been glorious times.

A shudder coursed through my body. I sensed a shifting in the magic realm, but it did not cause me to fear. Who could defeat me now? I took it as proof that the sword was on the move. It would come to Arthur soon, just as the shee witch told me it would. It would seek his hand as it always did, because the Pendragon blood ran in his veins, like it flowed through *my* body. And when it drew near, I would pluck it from him. Excalibur would finally be mine.

And with the sword in my hand, I would make everything right.

Chapter Six—Guinevere

I watched Morgan step outside the tavern and stare up at the starry sky; she seemed quite pleased with herself as she practically danced down the sidewalk. Once again, she ran ahead of me. Finding Arthur had proven easier than I expected. How could I have known that I would find him so close? But Morgan knew. She knew, and I had not. I was ashamed to admit that I had lost faith—I had wallowed in self-pity for nearly a century, and look what it had brought me. Morgan had the advantage, which was never a good thing. Morgan's pleasure always meant my destruction. She paused on the pathway, obviously perceiving a presence, but gave me no evidence that she either saw me or recognized me. Always too confident, too sure of herself. After a few moments, Morgan disappeared down a pathway and vanished around the corner of an old Tudor-style building. I felt her presence diminish, and then she was gone. I breathed a sigh of relief and quelled my anger. I had other things to think about now.

I wasn't familiar with the current layout of Cavanaugh, but I had been here before. Long ago. It was hours away from Saint James and had remained small and largely forgotten by the big cities to the east and south. I had made good time, but I sensed that dawn was merely a few hours away.

Yet, on my journey here, the echoes of the past called to me loudly; a broken monument here, an old pig trail turned road there. And the name of this place, the Questing Beast Tavern, stung me in ways I did not expect. Old King Pellinore, Elaine's father, spent his life in pursuit of the elusive Questing Beast. He had been devoted to his king, but once he encountered the beast, there was no reining him in. Many laughed at him behind his back—it had been an amusement at court—but Arthur had loved the old man, as we all did. The king had shown kindness and stopped the wagging of cruel tongues by giving Pellinore's Quest his blessing and charging the old king with ending the creature's mayhem. I assumed like everyone that Arthur sought to shield the old man from ridicule, but what if Pellinore knew something we did not? What if we'd all been wrong? Perhaps the Questing Beast had truly existed. I certainly wouldn't have believed in beings such as questing beasts or vampires or whatever type of enchantress Morgan had become until I joined their ranks. And now here I was, standing outside The Questing Beast Tavern and looking through a smudged window just as the poor used to peer through the windows of the keep when they wanted to have a peek at the Queen of Camelot.

Oh, if they could see me now! What would they say?

Long live the Undead Queen! Isn't that what Morgan called me?

I could not waste another second standing out here. I pushed open the tavern doors and slithered into a nearby booth to watch the small gathering. The bartender glanced in my direction, but I shook my head; with a disapproving look, he turned and walked the other way. Lucky for him.

Where are you, Arthur?

Oh yes, he was here—somewhere close by. The familiar rhythm, the essence of Arthur was here! I closed my eyes and felt around the room with my mind. I was sure this modern-day Arthur would not have the memories that I had. None of his previous incarnations remembered who they were save one. What would I see in him now? Would it be as Morgan said? Did he look much the same? Perhaps this had been a mistake...but then again, Morgan already knew he was here. There was no need to hide him away from her. Whatever her reasons, she had left him behind tonight.

My vampire's heart surged with hunger, and I dug my fingernails into the palms of my hands to keep myself under control while I searched for him. It had been a mistake to forego my feeding. By tomorrow night, I would be ravenous. There were only seven souls here, and two were outside. One would have thought I would know Arthur immediately, but I was cautious, careful. Uncertain.

Sometime in the last century, Arthur had indeed returned and had known, fully known who he was. I watched him closely because he grew up so near to me, so near to where Camelot once stood. It was as if the Once and Future King had truly returned to drag the world back into the light. That Arthur had the same hazel eyes and the shock of blond hair that young Arthur used to have and that our children had. But that boy, my Arthur returned, unfortunately died from a sudden fever, never knowing who I was and never knowing that I was so nearby. But then again, how could a ten-year-old child ever understand what I wanted to tell him? And when he died I had pledged to never seek out my husband again. To never search. Perhaps it would be better even now that I should turn and look the other way. Even now I should leave and not come back...but then I found him. He sat at the bar, his back turned to me. He wore blue jeans and a dirty t-shirt. He was muscular and tall, and I could sense that his mind was full of worry.

Arthur!

The rest of these minds, the ones that weren't soaked in alcohol or obsessed with some horrible secret, were easy to decipher. As he had been when we were alive together, Arthur was now a complex mess of emotions; he wore his character and his feelings on his shoulders just as he used to wear his armor. He was facing a dilemma, one that I did not fully understand, but just seeing him made me clutch my palms into fists in amazement. *This was my Arthur—just as he had been, handsome and strong and intelligent.* I would know him anywhere, and if I could have, I would have wept. But if I knew him, he would also know me and remember. A sudden fear came over me. My goal had been to come here, to seek him and find him, to make contact with him, but I was not prepared to do so now. Oh, to be this old and still be such a coward. Yet, I could not leave Arthur untouched. I could not allow Morgan to have the last evil word whispered in his ear. With my eyes closed, I spoke his name softly.

"Arthur..."

And then I opened them, half expecting to see him standing before me.

Oh, how I love you, Arthur!

But the man at the bar had not moved. He remained on his stool and tossed back the remnants of his drink, all the while staring at the fuzzy television screen. Sadness washed over me. Yes, it was him, but only the beginning of him. He did not know who he was—he did not yet remember.

And that was unfortunate. I frowned at no one in particular.

Arthur! You must remember!

What was my plan now? What should I do? Wait until he stepped outside and explain it all to him? The thought of speaking to him stoked my fear, and then my hunger gnawed at me. Could I trust myself with him? That was not a feasible plan of action. Not at all, not as long as Excalibur was in danger—not as long as Arthur was in danger. My hunger grew. I would find nothing here that would help me, but I knew him now. Then I heard someone say his name. *Luke Ryan.* I repeated his name, and he half turned in his stool and glanced in my direction. Oh no! Now he would see me. He would see me and be repulsed! Feeling conflicted, I slid out of the booth and left the tavern without delay. If I flew and used all my remaining energy, I would make it back to my kistvaen, but I would have to feed first thing tomorrow. Yes, I must go!

Morgan had been here. Arthur was here, and somewhere close there was yet another, someone else I once knew, but tonight was not the night for reintroductions. I could not face Arthur. Not yet, not like this. For when he knew who he was, he would remember who he had been, what I had done. I had sipped the vial and sought to die like a coward. I had not fought for Camelot. I had not fought for Lochlon or Alwen. I had failed Arthur.

He would know what I had become.

Without a sound, I disappeared into the darkness. Arthur followed me to the door but went no further. No, I would never make it back to the tower tonight. I would have to seek sanctuary elsewhere.

It was strange to think as I sailed through the streets that I had never felt more alone. Unwilling to draw attention to my presence in the sleepy town, I withdrew into a cellar. I barred the door with whatever furniture I could find and took sanctuary in a windowless inner room. Not strong enough to seek out Arthur with my mind again, I consoled myself with the knowledge that he was close. Closer than he had been in a very long time.

Despite Morgan's intentions, I could not prevent a sliver of hope from rising up within me.

Perhaps this was my chance to redeem myself! Maybe I could make everything right again or at the very least tell Arthur how much I loved him—how I had never stopped loving him. How sorry I was that I had failed him.

As the sun began to rise, I closed my eyes and found him in my dreams.

Chapter Seven—Guinevere

1260

With a mouth full of apple and the sun on my face, I lay back in a field of clover and closed my eyes in complete satisfaction. The stolen treats were not any ordinary apples but rare golden ones that grew in the priests' orchards. Sweeter apples I had never tasted, even sweeter because they were stolen. No one could climb a wall faster than I, the Maid of Cameliard, the daughter of Leodegrance or the Lion, as some called my father. Although I had done this many times, for the property was adjacent to my father's lands, today I would be found out for my crimes against the monks who loved to keep records of such things.

Apparently, stealing apples was so serious a crime that the priests sent an enforcer that day. As I opened my eyes to stare up at the glistening sunlight that filtered through the apple trees above me, I searched for the sun. But it was not where I expected it to be. In its place was the face of a young man with sparkling hazel eyes. He blotted out the sun, and the effect created an otherworldly halo around his fair-haired head.

"My Lady Guinevere, I have come to ask you about some apples." His voice was tinged with amusement, either at me or at his task, but he kept a polite and warm tone.

I sat up immediately and defiantly took another bite of the fruit before tossing the core behind my shoulder. When I finished chewing, I challenged him, "What apples?"

"Those, I think," he said, pointing at the remnants. "That is, if I were to believe that you would commit such a crime. Stealing apples from a priory seems quite beneath you, Lady Guinevere. What would your father, King Leodegrance, say about this behavior?"

"Crime? There has been no crime, sir. These orchards were ours until recently. I forgot that he deeded my orchards to the brothers here." The lie came easily, but I could not hide the warmth I felt in my face. "May I ask who you are and how it is you climbed that stone wall so quickly? I only just came here myself."

To my complete surprise, the young man picked a golden apple from off the ground beside me, tossed it up in the air and caught it. "I have been following you, lady. I have to admit, your climbing skills are very impressive, almost as good as my own. Although I freely admit that I may have the advantage, for I have not had to climb anything wearing a skirt. It must be quite a challenge."

"I find that hard to believe." I sat up even taller, feeling a little aggravated that my privacy had been encroached upon by this stranger.

"Why is it so hard to believe that I appreciate your athleticism and your skill for climbing walls like a Welsh man?"

"No, not that. I do not believe that you have never climbed in a skirt. With such lovely blond hair and unusual eyes, I would think you well suited for skirts."

My insult did not bring the results I expected. The young man threw back his head and laughed and then sat beside me in the sweet-smelling grass. "You have a quick wit, Lady Guinevere."

His amusement did not ease my nerves as he seemed to suppose it would. "And you are quite the rude one, speaking to me without introducing yourself. Or do they not believe in proper introductions where you come from? It must certainly be from well north of here."

"Oh, they do believe in those rules where I come from. In fact, everything I do is wrapped around some sort of protocol. Hence my reason for climbing the wall. I too sought escape." His answer surprised me, and I suddenly felt quite sorry for him. There was the sound of true resignation in his voice and a surprising weariness for someone so young. How old was he? Surely not much older than I. I surveyed him carefully as I chewed on another apple. No, I did not know him, nor did he appear familiar to me in face or figure, but I refused to ask his name. He was the one who had broken the solitude of my orchard, after all.

"I grow weary of formalities, but that is no reason to be rude to you. Forgive me, Lady Guinevere." He lay back in the grass, making himself comfortable in my presence. Unsure what to do, I flicked a strand of red hair out of my face and continue to chew on my stolen fruit. I had not completely lied to him. This orchard had been in my father's possession until he deeded it to the church. I was as devout as anyone in our family, but I loved this orchard and resented that my father had so freely given away this treasure without consulting me. Cameliard had belonged to my mother, and now that she was dead it seemed my father took joy in selling off bits of her property. First the small castle at the edge of Lyoness and now the orchards, including my favorite one. It was as if he wanted to forget all about her.

I had heard the rumors—that my father had another wife—but I liked to pretend that they were not true. And I liked to pretend that my mother was watching over me here. Even now. What would she say about me being alone in the orchard with a strange young man who had the boldness to assume a position of superiority over me, the daughter of King Leodegrance?

"What now, sir? Are you here to arrest me?" I was curious about the stranger but refused to demand his identity. Doing so would drag him back into the formalities he seemed eager to be rid of. I understood that. But I did want to know what his intentions were for me. I felt no danger, but one could never tell with these highborn lads. Their collective sense of entitlement irritated me. Yet, I wasn't sure the blond-haired young man beside me was highborn at all. He had an unusual way about him; he was certainly educated, as I could tell by the way he spoke and moved. But these were uncertain times.

"If they come to arrest you, Lady Guinevere, they will have to arrest us both, for I too am enjoying these stolen fruits. But I think that..."

And then I heard voices calling—worried voices.

"Where is he? He was just here! You and you—look there! Where could he have gone to?"

The young man beside me stood up and tossed the rest of his apple into the grass far away beside my own remnants, and I did the same with the last of the evidence. I wiped the juice from my face with the back of my hand and stared at him questioningly. Tilting my head, I gave him a hard appraisal and asked, "Are they looking for a criminal? Besides me?"

"No, lady." He wiped the grass off his tunic and held out his tanned hand to me. "They are looking for the king."

His answer surprised me. "The king? Which king?"

"This one." He patted his chest and bowed his head slightly. "I am Arthur. Come, Lady Guinevere. We might as well leave the peace of the orchard; they will not cease to search for me. Unless you wish that I leave you to face the brothers alone."

"God forbid," I said with a grin as he helped me to my feet. I was completely surprised and completely in love with Arthur Pendragon.

Chapter Eight—Luke Ryan

By the time I headed home, I understood how far I had exceeded my alcohol limitations. Luckily for me, my place wasn't that far from the tavern, so I caught a cab after Buddy abandoned me. After fumbling with the keys to the flat for an eternity, I managed to stumble indoors and collapse on the couch. I think I called for Michelle once or twice, but she never appeared. Just as well. She hated it when I got drunk. And she probably hated me now that I had pulled a no-show for our anniversary dinner. If I had the energy and the room would stop spinning furiously around me, I might take a peek in the bedroom closet. If her clothes were gone, she was gone. Michelle didn't love anyone as much as she loved her clothes. She'd left me twice before; each time was a surprise, but the telltale sign had always been the empty hangers.

Oh, to hell with it. I would think she would understand after the day I had. Surely she knew about it. The explosion rocked the whole damn town!

The sad truth was, Michelle wanted something from me that I couldn't give her. She had long, tanned legs, which I loved, a wide, sexy smile and all kinds of brains...but I didn't love her, and I couldn't say why. I felt I ought to. She wanted me to—hell, I wanted to—but I didn't. I couldn't. Oh, I knew what love was...I had been in love before, with Charlene Townsend when we were in high school, but it didn't last. Relationships with me never did.

Why am I thinking about this now? I need sleep. I want to forget this day ever happened.

And I dreamed, which was rare for me. I was one of those people who only dreamed when I had a fever, and it was always something crazy like some dark invisible force chasing me or a strange creature clawing at my flesh. Lots of people received insights from their dreams, or so Michelle explained to me once—she believed in all that therapeutic nonsense, but I had never been one to put much stock in dream symbols and whatnot. I believed only in things I could see and understand.

I dreamed I stood in a high place, like a tower. I could feel the wind rushing around me, and beneath me I heard the sound of water. Was I falling into the water? I could hear voices whispering urgently around me, but I couldn't make out what they were saying. They spoke over one another; the urgency in their whispers was clear. And—I knew them! I believed that, *knew* that. They whispered at me again and again, wanting me to respond to them, but I could not quite understand what they demanded of me. *What do you want?* I yelled in my dream. A fog gathered around me, and emanating from the haze I heard the sounds of swords clashing, horses' hooves pounding the ground, men screaming in anger and pain—and I wasn't in that high place anymore. Now I was in a field, a muddy field. The unearthly fog gathered even closer, and in front of me stood a young man. The fog covered his face, but his name was on the tip of my tongue. As it almost fell off my lips, dread rose up in me and chilled me to the bone. And then someone shook me and shook me hard.

"Hey! You're going to be late. Come on, I've got coffee ready." My gnomish friend Buddy was stirring in my tiny kitchen, and I detected the smell of coffee brewing. I sat up on the couch and rubbed my head, wondering where I was and why the hell I had drunk so much the night before. My mouth felt dry and my heart heavy, and then I remembered. *Markie!*

"Hey! What's going on? Any word?" I rubbed my eyes and tried to get up but decided I needed to take things slow for a minute or two.

"He pulled through the night, and it's looking like he's going to do just fine. That's one tough kid." Buddy walked into the living room holding two cups of coffee. I accepted one and stared into the dark brew with swollen eyes.

I breathed a sigh of relief. "Well, that's good to hear. I don't know how that's possible, but I'm not going to look a gift horse in the mouth. The kid took a pounding." What a punishing hangover!

Buddy nodded his head in agreement, his eyes wide as he sipped from the chipped mug. "You ready for today? I have no doubt it will be a long one for you."

"I'm sure I'll have a lot to answer for when I get to work. McAllister is going to give me hell. I should have used the robot."

"Hindsight is twenty-twenty, Ryan. But you know I have your back. The whole crew does. This isn't something we can't overcome." I took another sip of the scalding liquid. "You want some breakfast? Or is that pushing things?" Buddy grinned at me. "You really tied one on last night."

Then I remembered he had left me high and dry. "Where did you disappear to? One minute you were there, and the next you were gone. Did I out-drink you?"

Buddy's smile vanished, and he said, "The place was getting too crowded. You know I don't like crowds." He was a private guy, and I didn't really know much about him other than the few details he offered in passing. Strange thing was, I felt as if I had known him for longer than I actually had. I took him at face value, just as he did me, and we worked well together. He had no family, kind of like me, and over the years of working at three different mines together, we sort of adopted one another. He was the closest thing I had to family.

"Just a minute, are you saying that you couldn't hang with the young dog?" My feeble attempt at pretending to be jovial didn't really lighten the mood, but I had to give it a shot.

Buddy raised his furry eyebrows and narrowed his dark brown eyes. "I admit nothing; I just had some business to attend to." That pretty much meant he didn't want to talk about it, and I was too tired and hung over to push him. Whatever it was, he would tell me about it eventually.

"Let's get going, Ryan. Quarter till eight now, and I'm sure Wayne is gonna want to see you first thing. You'll have reports to fill out. About a thousand, I suspect."

"Yeah, I'm sure." I slugged down as much of the hot coffee as I could stomach, spent a few minutes tidying up in the bathroom, changed into a clean shirt, grabbed my gear and walked out with Buddy. We took his old rust bucket of a van to the Cavanaugh Mine, which was about a half mile past the Questing Beast. The mine sat up the ridge, and behind it were the Perilous Mountains. I had no idea who named them that, but the moniker was appropriate. More than one group of hikers had gone missing from up in that area. I groaned when I saw the many OSHA vehicles in the parking lot.

"Damn," I muttered to myself. I knew this was going to happen, but the response was quicker than I expected. Buddy put the van in park, set the parking brake and stared at me pitifully.

"I'm glad it's you and not me."

Sighing in frustration, I answered, "That's helpful. I wish it was you and not me. Well, I wish none of this had ever happened."

"There wasn't anything you could do about it, Ryan. Sure, you could have waited for the robot, but McAllister wouldn't have liked that one bit. In fact, I'm pretty sure he would have said no. He doesn't like bringing in the expensive equipment unless he absolutely has to. In his mind, it wouldn't have made a difference. Besides, Mark Wheeler wanted to go, and you couldn't have stopped him even if you wanted to. The accident was an unlucky strike. In this business, you blow things up...and sometimes people get hurt. No amount of preparation and security checks would have prevented this. Trust me, I've been digging holes for as long as I can remember, and I've seen more than one guy lose a limb or his life. Markie didn't lose either. He is luckier than most, and he will recover. Don't let them push you around."

"Thanks, counselor," I muttered as I climbed out of the van and headed to the "grill," as we sometimes referred to the administration office. I visited the grill about once a week to sign off on those electronic time cards and file any necessary incident reports. Unfortunately, this week there would be a huge one. To my surprise, Buddy followed me inside as I stepped into the shack and faced what looked like a firing squad of unhappy strangers camped out around McAllister's desk. Wayne McAllister was never in a good mood, and this morning was no exception. But who could blame him? I blew up part of the mine and almost killed one of the miners yesterday. If I was him, I'd fire me.

"You're late," McAllister announced as he shoved around a stack of paperwork and waved me to a grimy chair, the only chair available. He gave Buddy a *what the hell are you doing here?* look but didn't order the old man out. I was kind of glad I didn't argue with him about the time; I was clearly not late, but McAllister had other fish to fry, most notably the

OSHA folks who'd heard about yesterday's mishap. I removed my hat and sat in the chair, waiting for the axe to fall where it may.

"You know everyone, I think." I nodded in agreement even though I only knew half the people here. Less than half, actually. No time for reunions, either. I wanted to hear what they all had in mind for me. "I spoke with Mark Wheeler's father this morning."

"Norman?"

"Yeah. The senior Wheeler plans to sue the mine for what happened to his kid. You should never have let him in there, Ryan. Uncorking that explosive was your responsibility, and you shrugged it. You blinked, and it will cost us all."

"That's bull! Markie begged me to let him go. He's part of the crew, McAllister. He wanted to earn his chops. I cannot believe Norman would sue the mine. Are you sure? He was there with me, for God's sake."

McAllister looked down his nose at me as I were a bug he'd like to squash, but I continued. "It was an accident, clear and simple. Norman encouraged me to allow Markie in. I know I took a risk that I shouldn't have taken. I agree it should have been me, but I swear I would never have sent him in there if I had known this was going to happen!"

McAllister pulled on his tie. He looked like a man who was being strangled by his own suit. He rose to his feet and towered over me, all 6-foot-5 of him. I stood up too—no way was I going to let the guy stand on top of me. "You said it yourself: it should have been you. You had no business allowing a greenhorn to deal with that dud."

I shrugged, refusing to be dominated by McAllister and his pack of wolves. "Right! I got it, but the kid wanted to go in. It's not like he had never been trained on it, like he'd never seen explosives before. Mark Wheeler was Class Three Certified! He wanted to move up. He begged me to give him a shot, so I did."

"I don't care if he got on his hands and knees and kissed your damn feet. He should never have been the one going in. You handle the duds, Ryan. That's always been the deal, and any mine boss knows it. And for God's sake, we have a robot...why wasn't the robot used?"

"You know why, Wayne. It's not always easy to get that robot here. It would have taken an act of Parliament to get it approved; you and I both know you wouldn't have waited. I only did what you expected me to!"

Some of the suits shifted in their expensive shoes—I'd all but called McAllister out in front of them. They didn't intervene but listened and cast a wary eye in McAllister's direction. "That's bull, and you know it! And here's another thing, were you using Triton caps?" McAllister tossed a melted yellow stick on the desk. A few of the women on the OSHA team gasped, but they should've known the thing was empty. Not even a fool like McAllister would have tossed a stick of dynamite on the desk.

"I don't know what that is or where it came from. We always use ammonium nitrate."

McAllister's typically pink face reddened as he glanced around the stuffy room. One man cleared his throat while the woman beside him glared at me. They clearly didn't believe me, for whatever reason. Or they didn't want to. "That's not what Norman Wheeler says. He says this could've all been prevented. So he's suing us, and the mine will shut down during the investigation. God knows how long that will be! You are out, Ryan." He sat back down, leaned back in his leather chair and blasted an excruciating glower in my direction. I couldn't believe what I was hearing.

Buddy sputtered, "Wait a minute, McAllister! You're not listening. I was there, and I know what I saw—and I know what I used. Nobody uses old crap like that, and nobody made that kid go in there. He demanded to go, and Ryan gave him a shot."

McAllister raised his hand. "Look, Moran, I'm sure there will be plenty of time to have this out in court, but this is how it is for now. You're off, Ryan. And Moran, you're on. Or do I need to hire somebody else?"

Buddy stood with his hands on his hips, looking at me and then at McAllister. "You are doing this guy wrong, Wayne. This isn't how we do things around here. It was an unpredictable event, a complete accident. That's why they call them accidents! This was not something anyone could foresee. Mark Wheeler wanted to go into that mine, and into that mine he went."

I scrunched my hat in my hands. "No, he's right, Buddy. It was my responsibility. I knew the risks. I'll go peacefully, McAllister. Buddy is more than capable to lead the mine."

"The guys aren't going to like this, Ryan," Buddy complained.

"Speaking of which, I'm telling you to steer clear of the crew, Ryan. The legal team," he said, waving to the three suits on the left of his desk, "they want to keep the other miners out of this case as much as they can. If you go chatting with them, it might be believed that you're asking them to cover for you. So you'll have to avoid contact with the crew, at least until this thing blows over."

"Well, if you're firing me, I'm pretty sure it's not going to blow over. I'm done, right? You can't tell me who I can and can't talk to." Beads of sweat popped out on my forehead. The combination of stress and last night's boozing was wreaking havoc on my body.

"We sure as hell can if we're paying for your legal representation," McAllister snapped back.

One of the men beside him spoke. "I think we should just start over with a local crew, Mr. McAllister. It is time for a change. Let's put in people that know this area. No offense to our American miners who are a long way from home on this job, but it is time to get some good union guys in here. It might go a long way toward repairing relationships with the locals."

McAllister didn't answer him, but he did nod once as if to say he'd consider it. "Moran? It's now or never. What are you going to do?"

I headed out the door and left them to haggle over it by themselves. I had no ill will toward Buddy, but I did not want to be part of this conversation. I should've known I could not leave him behind—he was dogging my heels in seconds.

I put my hand on his shoulder and said, "You take care of the place, my friend. The crew needs you. I'll leave peacefully. McAllister knows I'm sorry for what happened to Markie, but I did things by the book. You know I did. I always have. All the same, the accident happened...and I was the guy in charge." I was fuming, but I was also sorry for what happened to Mark.

"Where do you think you're going? I'm not taking that job. No way, no how. McAllister should stick by you, not throw you under the bus. If he would do that to you, I know he'll do that to me. Where you go, I go too."

Some of my crew pulled up, and I was eager to get out of there. McAllister had been right about one thing—I couldn't put those guys in a worse situation. I waved at them but didn't slow down despite their calls. It made me sick to leave them wondering what the hell was going on, but what choice did I have? "You gonna give me a lift home?"

"Yeah, climb in."

No, this was wrong. I couldn't leave these guys in the lurch. I felt like I was abandoning the crew, and I just couldn't do it. "Stop the van, Buddy. This isn't right."

"Hey, you heard what McAllister said."

"I don't give a damn what he said. I'm talking to my guys."

He shook his head and clutched the gearshift forward with a lurch. "Not this time, Ryan. Leave them out of the fight for now. Call them later when you have your head together. Right now, you're mad, they'll be mad and none of you are thinking clearly."

From the rearview mirror, I watched the crew wave at us to stop. Buddy didn't waver. He clutched one more time, and we turned the corner and left the Cavanaugh Mine behind.

It was the worst feeling in the world.

Chapter Nine—Guinevere

My increasingly cold skin and the excruciating pain in my abdomen warned me that I dared not postpone my next kill much longer. My sleep had been interrupted multiple times; the cellar had not been a good idea, but at least I had not been discovered. I came home at first dark only to climb into my kistvaen to steal a few more minutes of rest, but I could wait no longer. Climbing from the stone box, I almost doubled over from the ache that soared through my body.

Arthur, how will I ever help you? I am a murderous heap of blood and bones. I am nothing, my love. Nothing like you remembered me.

Glancing down at my hands, I could see that I had indeed fasted far too long. My skin sagged slightly, and my normal paleness began to display a subtle shade of blue. I could not avoid feeding tonight; I needed my strength for what lay ahead of me. Feeding must take priority over all else. What good would I be to my husband if I allowed myself to become a withered husk? How would I protect him if I was as weak as a kitten? His handsome face passed through my mind. I remembered him battle-weary and gaunt but always strong. Strange to think that he would need me to protect him when the reverse had always been true. Arthur had been my protector, until he could not be, and then Lancelot had. With purposeful intention, I forced them both from my memory.

The building beneath me had grown quiet earlier than usual, which told me it must be Friday, the day when most left the Wells building not long after lunch to enjoy mortal frivolities. Normally I would never feed here, but my hunger was palpable and I had allowed myself to waste away. How was I to know how things would change? How easy it would have been to slip away into nothingness and abandon this life, this horrible blood-filled life. I knew now that was what I'd had in mind, but I could not. I had subconsciously decided to starve, but that was before Arthur returned to me. Now I had waited too long.

Instinctively, my ears searched for sounds of human activity. I quickly found a suitable target.

Ah, Carlos! I have long waited to meet you!

At least now I had a choice about whose blood I drank. Those first few nights after Morgan's curse had been hell. Fleeing from Avalon, I made my way through the water and into the small village of Barton. I did not know what drove me there, but I wasted no time satisfying the blood lust Morgan had awakened in me. And when the gorging was over, when the village had fallen silent, I woke from my feverish rampage horrified at the evidence left on my hands. Morgan's laughter mocked me as the body of a child slipped from my hands onto the ground with a dull thud. And as those lingering rays of the sun hung on the horizon, threatening to burst across the sky, terror rose within me. As the sky brightened, the fear of it, the absolute revulsion of the light overwhelmed the shame of my blood gorging. I began to scream. My despair was complete.

And then she was there—Nimue, my merciful rescuer! Her angular face was a mask of calm as she threw her voluminous green cloak over my body, shielding me from the sun, and together we fled from the field and into the woods. Once the surge of blood subsided, the horrors of my crimes returned in full force. I heard again the cries for mercy, the muffled whimpering of the people whose lives I had ended that night. Yes, I had done horrible things.

"Kill me, Nimue! Kill me!" I begged the healer.

With a sad, distant expression she said, "You will not die, my queen, although you will wish for death many times." Feeling the sun burning through the cloak, I clutched her hand as she led me into a dark cave. We moved deeper into the cave, and Nimue disappeared and reemerged with a candle. I could not believe what I saw. What I thought was a damp hole was actually a beautifully appointed room illuminated now by the glow of a single candle. Some magic, perhaps? Soft light shimmered around the room, and I whimpered at the sight of it. "False light, my queen. It will not harm you. A trick only. See the mirrors? They make the light bounce. You must rest, Guinevere. Rest now."

I grabbed her arms and clung to her desperately. I could feel the dried blood caking on my skin; the smell of it sickened me. "You do not know what I have done."

"You have fallen under Morgan's curse. You must remain here; remain hidden from the sun and from everyone living. Change your clothes and toss them outside the cave. I will burn the soiled garments for you. I fear that if you do not obey me, the dogs will come and find you. They will certainly come looking for the one that..." Her voice trailed off.

"Nimue, what have I done? It feels like a horrible nightmare. Tell me the truth! Only that, a night-mare?"

Her sad expression revealed the truth. No, it had been not a horrible dream but reality. "Remain here, my queen. Remain hidden far in the back, past that table. You see the entrance? No light will penetrate there, and no one will see it." I did see an entrance—one I hadn't seen before. I suddenly felt exhausted, as if the world were crashing in around me. "Do you understand me?"

I felt so strange, tired yet invigorated in a devilish way. Although I had done evil, I wanted more. Perhaps if I could have wept, if I could have shed a tear, I would have been able to repent, to have been absolved of the curse. But no tears came. I would discover later that I would never cry again.

Nimue rose to her feet, and instinctively I grabbed her. She whimpered in pain, but I could not bring myself to release her. "Guinevere, let go of me. I will help you if you let me." I finally did as she asked; I stared at my hands wondering how this had happened. My instincts were so taut I felt like a prowling cat, a creature of the darkness ready to pounce on anyone around me. "I am your friend, Guinevere." I nodded and sat in the wooden chair nearest me, then watched as Nimue shuffled through a trunk. What would happen when she left me alone? Would the demons within me rise up again and demand more blood?

"You cannot leave me..." I whispered desperately. "Do not leave me alone, for I cannot trust myself. There is something in me, Nimue. A shadow...it is death, I think."

Nimue handed me a green dress, simply made and soft to the touch. I recognized it as one of her own. She had worn the garment to court the few times she came recently, and now she placed it in my hands. I noticed that she did not touch me.

"Listen to me. Clean yourself up; you will find water over there. Change your garments and then put them outside so I may burn them. Then go rest; hide in the darkness. I will return before the sun sets."

Feeling like one who walked in a dream, I did as she asked me. I washed my body with the icy cold water and put on her dress, then I rolled my soiled clothing up into a bloody ball and tied it with a piece of string I found in a cupboard. Tossing the wad of clothing out of the cave as far as I could without putting myself in the light, I retreated to the hidden room and somehow fell into a deep sleep. I did not dream that first night.

Nimue returned near dark and explained to me the horrible curse that I had fallen under. "You are *leanan shee*, my queen. Tell me what happened. How is it that you came to drink the blood of the shee?"

"But those are just tales! This can't be true!" Without tears but with deep shame, I confessed to Nimue what I had done. I told her everything: that I, in a moment of cowardice, drank the vial offered to me thinking that I would slip away peacefully, perhaps to join Arthur. And I did receive death, of a kind. In that, the maid who offered me the vial had kept her promise. Little did I know she was Morgan's servant. Nimue told me what I knew already—my decision to take my own life had put me in greater mortal peril; it cost me my humanity. I was now Morgan's creature. The same frenzy would overwhelm me every night, and I would be a slave to the blood lust for as long as I lived.

Nimue lingered with me for a season, long enough to show me how to control the madness that threatened to kill the last bit of Guinevere, Queen of Camelot. With her knowledge of shee lore, my only companion set about trying to unwind the curse or at least set me free from the constant, nightly need for blood, but to no avail. One evening she came to me and said, "This is a magic of a degree beyond mine. It is darker, craftier. I will continue to seek an answer, but I am afraid I must leave you for a while. Merlin will know its source; I am sure of it. I must find Merlin."

In my wretchedness and rage, I charged at her. How dare she abandon me for Merlin, the betrayer of us all! He'd left us when we needed him the most. Furthermore, he had never been my friend, and I had no illusions that he would help me now. My anger and hunger gave the madness a foothold in my soul, and with my teeth bared and nearly out of my mind, I surrendered completely to my inner demon. We struggled, but Nimue subdued me with a simple spell; when I came to myself, I agreed with her that we must part ways. Nimue could no longer help me, nor did I wish to bring her harm. So I remained alone, never knowing what became of her in that life or the next, for she never returned to me. I did not fault her for that.

But Carlos...he was another matter. Him I would bring much harm—with no regret. His blood released from his body would solve two problems. His death would rid the world of a diabolical criminal and bring me sustenance.

I stepped into the security guard's office without any notice. I watched him as he spied on others through his camera monitors. Strange to think that such a predator could be so easily stalked. When I tired of watching him, I purposely shuffled my feet to grab his attention.

"Who are you? How did you get in here?" Carlos tossed his empty potato chip bag on his desk and sprang from his office chair with his hand upon the baton at his waist. I smiled at his instinctual move.

Yes, he would recognize a predator.

Carlos stood a full foot taller than me; he had a muscular build, and I imagined some might think him handsome. *If they did not know of the worms that crawled in and out of his mind.* Despite his shiny silver-plated badge, he was an evildoer, a rare criminal with incredible potential. One day, if he was not stopped, he would kill many, beginning with Louise. I knew he had been planning the pink-haired housekeeper's death, and I had no reason to think he would stop with her, even though that one death was too many. I had grown to wish the suicidal girl would find some happiness. *How ironic that I, who had brought so much death, would take offense at one more.* Yes, Carlos had a crafty mind, but he was not crafty enough to outthink me and would not survive this encounter. I would have his blood. I would break my own rule to never kill near my kistvaen, but tonight would be my last night in my tower. I had to leave the Wells building. Perhaps it was fitting that I should go out in such a way.

I wore a blue satin dress with a modest hemline and a pair of silver heels. I had stolen this outfit from Louise's locker. After what I was going to do for her, I did not think she would begrudge me the dress. To Carlos, I appeared an innocent party girl, a young woman with long red hair, pale skin and expressive brown eyes. One who could be easily overpowered, and how he liked that. Little did he know that I could have slipped in at any time, tortured him and drunk his blood before he knew what was happening to him, but I wanted to enjoy this moment. Perhaps I had always known that someday I would do this. Carlos deserved to be toyed with, and I played with him like a cat played with a canary before she ate it.

"I said, how did you get in here? Are you deaf or drunk?"

"Through the door. You are Carlos, aren't you?"

As if he did not believe me, he walked to the door and twisted the knob. Seeing it was locked, he faced me with heightened scrutiny now. I did not sense fear yet, but it would come. I would make sure of that. Fear always made the blood taste better.

"I never leave this door open. Who gave you a key? Give it to me, young lady. Keys aren't supposed to be distributed to anyone outside the security team." He stretched his hand out to me, expecting a key to appear in it. Fool!

"Tell me, Carlos. Do you believe in a higher power? Do you believe in God?"

"What?"

"Do you believe in God? It is a simple question. Yes or no?"

He slid his key into the lock to open the door. And then I was there, right beside him. I moved faster than he expected, and finally I sensed his fear. It made me smile. He grabbed my arm, but I did not flinch or try to free myself from his grasp. His adrenaline and confidence surged.

"You believe in the devil, perhaps? Also a simple question. Yes or no?"

His grip on my arm tightened, and he paid no attention to my questions. Carlos was thinking about what to do with me. Should he expel me from the building now or call his superior? Or perhaps he should do something else. A glimmer of a smile crossed his face, but my chilly skin gave him pause. He withdrew his hand quickly as if he'd picked up a snake. I knew Carlos did not care for snakes, although he was one. A snake in human form.

"You need to leave. This area is off-limits to residents. Are you a resident?"

I shook my head and wagged my finger at him. "It is rude to answer a question with a question. I asked you two questions, and you have answered neither of them. Last chance." I drew closer to him; smelling his garlic-laced breath and cheap cologne did nothing to deter my growing hunger. Instinctively, Carlos drew back a foot or two, his hand on his baton again. I cleared the distance between us in a fraction of a second.

"Last chance, Carlos. God or devil? Which do you believe in?" Still, he gave no answer. His stupidity and growing fear were boring me quickly. "I know what you have planned, Carlos. You like to torture things, don't you? And oh, you like to watch things burn. You burned your mother's house down when you were twelve and blamed it on the neighbor." I plundered his mind even deeper. "You burned the woods behind your grandfather's farm and heard those animals screaming for help, but you did nothing." He gasped at hearing his secrets revealed, but I was not finished. "But that is not all, is it? You burned your wife's business down after she left you. Burned it down to the ground—you made her pay for her leaving. Nothing but ashes left, and even that was not enough for you; you plan to kill her, when you muster the courage. Is that why you plan to kill Louise? Are you building the courage to kill Mary?"

"What are you talking about? Who told you that?"

The scent of rising fear stirred my hunger. "This place...this building...you want to see it burn, don't you? And what about all the people who live here? Will you listen while they burn too?"

He let go of the baton and reached in his pocket for his knife. "Who told you that? Those are lies. Horrible lies!"

"Reach for that knife, Carlos. I want you to. Reach for it if you are man enough."

"I am plenty man enough to handle you, lady. Plenty!" He grinned and revealed the blade. I bared my teeth at him and reveled in seeing his expression change from one of confidence to one of total fear. I let loose a growl, my hands extended at my sides. He dropped his knife, and I was on him before he hit the ground.

He was dead in a few minutes. I rose from the ground feeling alive, rejuvenated and ready to take on Morgan.

Without bothering to move his corpse, I stepped over him and left my modern-day tower for the last time. I did not quake with fear at the implications. I had lived a long time, too long, and if my life was now required, so be it.

But I was not going to Arthur empty-handed.

A king would need his sword.

Chapter Ten—Luke Ryan

My mind said, "Get up, it's after seven," but my hangover argued that idea down. Two days in a row I had tied one on, but it was clear that this wasn't a viable solution to my problems. Despite McAllister's warning, I answered the phone when Pint called and told him about the meeting. He offered to speak up for me, but I told him not to bother. Cavanaugh wanted me gone, and that was that. I called Michelle a few times, but she didn't answer. I'd bet money her clothes were gone from the closet. I took the sound of the front door slamming as evidence that she had been here but was unable to rouse me. She never did have patience for me and my all-nighters. A few seconds later, I fell back to sleep, but it wasn't the blackout sleep I'd hoped for. It was something else.

Tap, tap, tap. Tap, tap, tap.

The sound—rhythmic, heavy, metal on metal—echoed in my ears. My skin tingled, and my heart banged in my chest. I experienced a major adrenaline rush but could not understand why or how. To calm myself, I took in air with my nose and forced it out my mouth. The air was so cold, it shocked my skin and excited me.

Tap, tap, tap.

This was the sound of strength, the sound of men preparing for battle. They collectively banged their sword hilts on their shields, a sound I had forgotten until I heard it again. A wet fog brushed my face and bare arms. I yelled in anger at the invisible enemy who lurked in the mist. Clutched in my hand was a sword—no, the sword of swords. My sword!

Usurper! The sword is mine... a threatening whisper mocked me, but I could not discern where it came from.

I growled in frustration, “Come out and face me! How dare you accuse me!”

Usurper...

Anger gripped me at the accusation. It was a familiar wound. Charging into the grayness, I spun and searched for my elusive enemy. The sound of swords crashing, the grunting and screaming of men in the throes of combat and the cries of the injured surrounded me. Yes, this was a field of death. I could feel myself sinking into the mud beneath me, and I swung the sword and shifted my stance to stabilize myself.

Usurper!

“Say that to my face! Stop hiding and fight me!”

Laughter filled my ears. It was light, feminine laughter but certainly not friendly. The laughter faded and became a growl.

“Who are you?” I demanded. “Speak now!” The sword vibrated in my hand as if warning me of the danger. Whoever this was, whoever challenged me, was approaching.

"Usurper, yield the sword to me and you will live. All your men will live. Let us end this now."

"Why should I give you what is mine? If you want the sword, come and take it," I yelled in the direction of the voice.

"Very well. I shall." As she stepped out of the mists, I beheld a slender figure—a young woman with long dark hair that hung loose over her shoulders stormed toward me. On her head rested a silver circlet, which sparkled dimly in the clearing air. She wore a long gray gown with a shimmering tunic of silver and a strange emblem upon the chest. A black crow, perhaps? No! A folded dragon! I spied no weapon at her side, no dagger, no sword, yet I sensed danger, as did my own sword. Yes, here was danger in its most raw and lethal form—the unseen. Seeing her eyes rest on my sword, I clutched it with both hands as if she might take it from me. Although I could tell she wanted it, she made no move to seize it from my hand. And she couldn't. The sword resisted her! The strange young woman stood quite peacefully with her hands clasped in front of her, a crimson, cold smile on her lips.

And then she began to whisper, and her words lingered in the air like frozen droplets of water. They floated toward me and flung themselves at my feet, pelting my shoes with ice. At first, I laughed at the trick. "Children's games," I muttered, but then my teeth began to chatter and my hands felt stiff. My legs grew weary and even threatened to fail me if I did not immediately move. With all my strength, I took a step away from her. The woman snarled and began to pace in front of me as she raised her voice and her pale hands, which had enchantments painted on them. Magic clung to me and filled the void in the air around me as the fog rolled back to reveal that my foe did not face me alone. Others stood with her. One in particular drew my attention.

A man stood behind her, a tall man encased in heavy armor. Although the woman's name eluded me, I knew his immediately. And as I spoke it, it filled me with dread.

"Mordred, raise your blade!"

He met my threat with a disdainful smirk but did not honor my challenge. He merely glanced at his companion. She spoke now, and her strange laughter had returned. "Good. Very good, Pendragon."

Despite the blast of cold that buffeted me, my forehead was damp with sweat. *Pendragon! Yes, I am the Pendragon!*

"What of me, brother?" she asked. "Do you know me, or have you forgotten me completely?" She clucked her tongue in mock disapproval. Someone called my name emphatically, again and again. They searched for me. My brothers in arms suffered without me. I must go to them! And I heard the name clearly now—my name.

Arthur! Arth-urrr...

"Arthur? I am Arthur!" My heart burned within me, testifying to this truth. Then extreme sadness fell on me like a heavy cloak. And I knew her name too.

“Morgan,” I whispered.

“Yes, finally,” she said in an exasperated tone. “Now, Mordred!” And as he charged at me, everything went black.

Chapter Eleven—Guinevere

Excalibur!

The thought sprang to my mind as I woke in the darkness of yet another a deserted cellar beneath an abandoned restaurant. It had been easy to find another hiding place in the city after I left my tower, as easy as sniffing for blood. I smelled no blood here, not even a trace of it, which confirmed that not a living soul dwelled here and that no one had been inside in a very long time.

I never questioned how I would find the sword after all these years. My hands had touched Excalibur, handled it on more than one occasion. The mystical blade was a mysterious thing, crafted by some ancient power trapped inside a fine steel edge. And once you made contact with it, you were forever changed. Knowing this, I refused to allow my daughter to handle the blade even momentarily—not even when the thing was wrapped in blankets. The Pendragon blood coursed through Alwen's veins, so maybe it would have been different for her, but it was her brother's destiny to wield it.

Too much heartache, too much unhappiness has sprung up as a result of too many hands on the sword.

I refused to allow a wedge such as the one lodged between Arthur and Morgan to penetrate the bond between Lochlon and Alwen. They must be true to one another, I believed, and my husband shared this hope. I had no idea why I feared such a division, but

I did. Down in my bones, I feared it. Morgan and Arthur had loved one another once too, until the struggle for Excalibur began. Until Arthur refused to recognize her as the Second Pendragon. Who had heard of such a thing, and why would Morgan believe Arthur would name her as heir when he had a son? Ah, the old wound. "How many hearts have you broken, Lancelot?" I had asked the knight once. He'd laughed uncomfortably at that comment but did not deny it. And he had wounded Morgan to her soul, or so I surmised. Why else would she hate me so staggeringly?

Later, sometime later, Arthur's sister had stolen Excalibur rather skillfully. Thanks to a loyal friend, her deception was soon discovered, but not before Arthur left for Camlann. Once I had the sword again, I knew what I had to do.

Excalibur must be hidden, for whoever held the sword ruled Britain.

Yes, the vultures at court were circling. Many in the court wanted to see how things would go at Camlann before declaring for me, but then they had circled even before Arthur went to battle. Lochlon's parentage was openly questioned now, accusations were made, and then word had come that my husband had been wounded on the battlefield. The false blade, Morgan's careful reproduction, had failed Arthur as Morgan knew it would. There was no time—I had no chance at returning Excalibur to him. And Arthur had not prevailed. Morgan's husband, a minor king named Accolon, had stolen Excalibur at her command sometime in the night, and it was only thanks to a faithful friend that we learned the true weapon's location so quickly. But it would do little good at Camelot when Arthur and Mordred were fighting at Camlann. The sword needed to return to Arthur's side, but who could I trust with such a task? Lancelot was with Arthur already, and I would not speak to Gawain since his accusations at the Round Table, even after his humble apology. No, the only thing I could do was hide the sword. If Arthur did not survive, it must go to Lochlon. This had always been Arthur's wish.

It had been night when Alwen and I rode out for the Church of Saint Albans. Fortunately, it was only an hour's ride from the keep; with all the confusion at court, it was ridiculously easy for the two of us to disappear. No one noticed us leaving.

Or so I had believed.

The brothers at Saint Albans did not question their queen's arrival. They believed me when I said Alwen and I sought a silent place to pray for the king. They offered to join us, but I demurely refused and pretended that the wrapped sword was a precious icon, too precious and rare to be revealed to anyone, save Alwen and myself.

Why now do you think of such things? It was not like me to ponder the past, but I had time to think as I lay on the dusty floor in a corner while the sun continued to retreat from the approaching darkness and all the creatures that dwelled within it. Including me.

Once upon a time, waking up in the blackness would have terrified me; indeed, I think it did drive me mad for a time, living in the shadows for long stretches, sometimes days and weeks. Surely that had been Morgan's goal, to drive me mad. I knew Morgan hated me, but I never set out to betray Arthur. Indeed, I had always been a faithful wife. But after the false news came that Arthur had fallen into the sea and was lost, I found comfort in Lancelot's arms.

I always knew Lancelot loved me, even before he married Elaine, but it did not matter then. I was pledged to Arthur, and I loved him deeply and with the heat of a thousand suns, to borrow a later phrase. But the grief that Lancelot and I shared over the loss of Arthur was great, and we found comfort with one another. Until Arthur returned.

Morgan had loved Lancelot too, even more than Accolon loved her. I suppose she saw my love for Lancelot as a betrayal, doubly so because of Arthur. But perhaps not. She hated her brother more every day for reasons I could not fathom. The sun disappeared, and the cellar became a vacuum of shadows.

Yes, darkness, my companion. Here I am.

I rose from the ground and dusted off my blue dress. I began removing the furniture from the doorway and I thought of my last friend, Nimue. If it had not been for Nimue and her knowledge of the secret shee cave systems, an ancient underground roadway hidden in the countryside, I would surely have perished either by the sun or at the hand of any number of knights who slowly acknowledged my unholy existence. Through the shee caves, I could cover great distances in a short amount of time; I could dwell in great darkness at temperatures not feasible for mere humans. In those first years, I wreaked havoc on the villages; I could not be stopped from taking blood when I needed it. In the beginning, I killed many. I traveled through the caves to escape capture many times and more than once dawdled late thinking that I would let the sun incinerate me into oblivion. But some invisible force, perhaps a sheer will to live, drove me to hide night after night. And so it had been for nearly seven hundred years.

And Nimue would come. She ignored my frothing mouth, my unintelligible ramblings. Nimue would speak my name and remind me of who I was, who I would be once again, and for a time I believed her.

Where are you, Nimue? So many have returned, but not you. Not you. Not Alwen. Not Lochlon.

I moved the hefty wooden table and paused before opening the door. Getting to the sword...that would be the tricky part. This place was much more crowded than it had once been, the streets narrower, more winding and confusing. But thankfully, the catacombs beneath old Saint Albans remained intact and unchanged. It had been Alwen's idea to hide the sword there in the catacombs. Sweet, lost Alwen. Like me, my daughter hoped that eventually the Lords of Britain would come to their senses and see that Lochlon was the true King after his father. But before she or I could return to claim the sword, Alwen was taken from me, stolen from my arms by an unknown kidnapper, surely at Morgan's command. Morgan must have believed that Mordred would be victorious at Camlann, that he would take Camelot, and then he would need a bride. What better way to solidify his hold on the throne than to marry Arthur's own daughter? It was a shrewd move and certainly the strategy Morgan would choose. She believed in the Old Ways. Take the queen—or in this case, the princess—and you win. Yes, a marriage to Alwen would have shored up Mordred's claim, but my nephew had not survived the battle.

And then what happened to my daughter? Morgan, I still intend to make you pay!

I shivered even now thinking about what may have happened to her.

Alwen used to come to me in my dreams and beg me to find her, to rescue her, but I had not been in my right mind in those early days. And then the dreams ended. Why had no knights searched for Arthur's daughter? Of course, many of them gave their lives for Arthur in that battle with Mordred. All those men of renown, brave knights who would gladly give their lives for the King, were now dead. And so was Alwen. She died without ever returning home. I failed her as well.

It was up to me alone to save Arthur from whatever evil plot Morgan's devilish mind had conceived. Clearly, she wanted Excalibur, as she had always lusted after it and the power that came with it. But the sword belonged to Arthur, and I had no doubt that it would know him in this new incarnation just as I knew him.

The sword would know him, and what better place for Excalibur than in the hands of the man for whom it was designed? With Excalibur, Arthur would defeat Morgan once and for all and I would be relieved of my duty as keeper of the sword. *It has been a heavy burden, Arthur. A heavy burden indeed.*

I pulled the door open and expected to flit down the alleyway unnoticed, but a figure blocked my way. And not a human figure.

Our eyes met, and even though his face had changed I knew who he was. I would know that penetrating stare anywhere.

Merlin!

Chapter Twelve—Guinevere

Lightning fluttered in the distance, illuminating the face of the ghost from my past. Moving faster than even I could, Merlin slipped past me into my temporary sanctuary. We did not speak but circled one another. I could not read his mind, even though I tried, and I got the distinct impression that he could not breach my mind either. Once we did our dance of power, I spoke first, anxious to learn the reason for his unexpected and unwelcome visit.

"It is true, then. Arthur has returned."

"Why do you ask me what you already know? Why else would you be in Saint Albans if not to retrieve the sword? There is nothing else here for you, except memories." His answer surprised me. To think that the Merlin of Britain would be standing in front of me now, I could hardly believe it.

"Memories are all I have now," I snapped back at him. "What do *you* have, Merlin?"

He appeared impatient with my question as always, or at least with me. I did not really wonder at his sudden and unexpected appearance at all. I knew Arthur had indeed returned, but I also knew there was no other reason for Merlin to seek me out except for Arthur's sake. And that infuriated me. Did that mean my husband's most trusted adviser had always known where to find me? Nimue and I had searched high and low for him before Arthur's battle at Camlann, but he was noticeably absent from all his usual haunts. And then when Arthur needed him the most, as the poison did its ugly work on him, Merlin again did not appear. It was almost as if he had given up on his pet project. Now here he was, ready to intervene once again on Arthur's behalf. What of mine?

"How did you find me?" I demanded from him.

"Does that matter?" He shrugged away the question as unimportant.

"It matters to me. What do you want from me, Merlin? Speak plainly—no double-talk. I have no patience for it...or you."

He stepped toward me in a challenging manner, and I watched his current façade melt away to reveal the Merlin I had known. Tall, with a toned physique and olive skin, Merlin gazed down at me as if I were a bug he would like to squash. He had a slightly aquiline nose, which further betrayed his Roman heritage, along with thick, dark hair and even darker eyes. A giant in his time, Merlin was no less imposing a figure now. The revealing made my heart sink. Yes, he had returned, and he had never been my friend.

"Plainly speaking, then, Queen Guinevere, Morgan has Arthur. And the king is at a disadvantage because he does not remember himself, not fully. He has been asleep a long time, but make no mistake...she will kill Arthur—after she toys with him a bit. She waits for you to offer her the sword."

"Morgan has Arthur?" My soul shrank at the news.

"Yes, and I am ashamed to say I could not prevent it."

A frown settled on my face. "Why? Is Morgan so strong now that you cannot stop her?"

Like before, Merlin did not answer the question I posed to him. It was that way with him. The conjuror never admitted his own failures, but he had a keen eye when it came to pointing out others' faults. Especially mine. "A partnership with me might be repugnant to you, but it is necessary to achieve our purpose."

How did he know what I intended to do unless he had been watching me? "All this time, you knew that I remained..." I almost said alive, but that was not what I meant. "You had to have known that Morgan's magic had worked its evil in me. You know what I am, what I can do, yet you never helped me. And Arthur, even after you abandoned him before Camlann...he lay dying still believing you would come, and yet you refused him your help." I raged at him and scratched at his face with my fingernails, leaving bloody cuts on his cheek. "You failed us, Merlin! Why would I trust you again?"

His face darkened as he shouted at me, "I never abandoned Arthur or you! I had no choice! There are many things in this world that are more powerful than I." Blood flowed down his face, and he made no effort to stop it. Instinctually, I sucked the blood from my fingernail, but it did not satisfy and I did not enjoy the taste. He narrowed his eyes and asked, "Did you meet the one whose blood you drank, or did Morgan give the blood to you another way? In wine, perhaps?"

My body felt cold, and the blood hunger returned as I stalled in giving him my answer. Not feeling particularly willing to tell him my shameful secret—that I tried to take my own life and failed miserably—I turned his question back on him. "Why do you ask what you already know?" Merlin's square jaw moved as his eyes narrowed. He was always one who kept his own counsel. Why should I confess my sins to him?

"I am not your judge, Queen Guinevere. You loved Arthur, of this I have no doubt, and it is that love I call upon now. But I must warn you that the danger to you has not ended." We stood in an eternal moment until a car horn blew down the street. The wind picked up outside, and the scent of rain rode the air. A storm would be good for me. I would be able to travel to the church without being seen. I wanted secrecy above all else.

"You call on the same love that you warned Arthur about? I will help Arthur myself!"

"For all your blood-fueled strength, Guinevere, you are not strong enough to defeat Morgan alone. And there are other obstacles as well. You will need my help—as I need yours." Of this I had no doubt. Merlin did need me, or else he would not have deigned to visit me this night.

"I find it ironic that you would ask me for help, as it was you who advised the Pendragon to choose another wife. The White Death, that is what you called me, if I remember correctly."

"Ill-chosen words, my queen. I saw, but I saw imperfectly. Stop fighting me! Or are you completely without human feeling now? Have you drunk so much blood, killed so many that you no longer have empathy or love, even for Arthur?" He reached for my hands and held them now. *He was strong, as strong as I!* "Guinevere, Queen of Camelot—wife of Arthur, it is to you I speak now."

For reasons unknown to me, his words sent shivers through my body and I found myself falling. I grasped at his clothes as I fell, and his strong hands caught me. I clung to Merlin as my body convulsed and confusion filled my mind. He stroked my hair and held me, and I eventually stopped shaking. Merlin whispered in my ear, "Perhaps it is not Arthur who needs to remember what once was, but you. You, Queen Guinevere, the Undead Queen and the Keeper of Excalibur." He whispered again to me, speaking kindly in the archaic Druid language he used when performing his work on the hills behind the keep. Memories of those long-ago days flooded my head. I could see Merlin standing before the Sacred Fire; I was there with Arthur, the antler-crown upon his head, and my maids heaped my arms with flowers.

Taking my head in both hands now, he looked into my half-closed, pain-filled eyes and whispered the sharp Druid words, "Remember, Queen Guinevere, wife of Arthur, mother of Lochlon and Alwen. You are the true and rightful wife of our Pendragon and

Queen of all Britain. You must come back to yourself, Guinevere. Remember everything."

Suddenly the room filled with light and Merlin vanished. My ladies laughed with delight as they ran toward me, wearing their wreaths of flowers and ribbons.

I had returned to Camelot!

Chapter Thirteen—Guinevere

After yesterday's wedding formalities, I was happy to hide away from the crowds that filled Camelot's many rooms and hallways. Arthur and I had not yet consummated our union—many of the king's advisers, of whom Merlin was chief, warned against our "joining" last night as the stars were not auspicious or some such thing. The news had not pleased my husband, who apologized profusely in private, but I put his mind at rest. I could wait for him another day. Or a hundred if required. He liked that answer and assured me that I would have to wait only one more night. I did not know how to respond, so I kissed his hand and allowed him to kiss my cheek. I could still feel his lips on my skin. How could I deny that I wanted him as hungrily as he desired me?

Needing a distraction, I spent the morning playing with a feisty kitten I had rescued from a castoff basket earlier in the week. I laughed at his antics as I teased him with a bit of yarn, but my mind traveled elsewhere. Such a strange yet deeply moving affair, my wedding to the Pendragon. Arthur had been dressed in a soft green tunic with tan breeches and soft leather boots, and on his head was a crown of gold. All things went as I expected until the sword was revealed. Until the moment I was asked to kiss the blade. That was the first time I encountered true magic. The touch of steel on my lips sent a shock through me, and I saw Arthur smile. My eyes widened as we then kissed—the most chaste of kisses, of course. It was as if I married not only Arthur Pendragon but also Excalibur.

"Come now, Queen Guinevere. You cannot postpone this forever. We have to dress your hair and prepare you for tonight!"

"Very well," I agreed, trying to sound bored with the whole thing. With the evening would come my wedding night, and I would no longer be simply the daughter of a minor king. I would be the queen of Britain, the High Queen. My fingers shook as I tied a bow around the black kitten's fuzzy neck, and I watched as the ridiculous creature tried to free himself from his silky prison. I felt a bit like the kitten. Although I found Arthur appealing in every way and loved him, the events swirling around me left me feeling powerless. But this was my fate. I would be High Queen even though I never dreamed this for myself. Before me, there had never been a High Queen in Britain except for Arthur's mother, Igraine, and she had reigned only briefly.

The black ball of fur growled at the end of the ribbon. He rolled it into a ball and chased it repeatedly. Feeling merciful, I tugged at the ribbon and set him free. I decided then and there that I would name him Sir Spitfire and that he would go with me on my journey. I would insist on it. As he pounced on the ribbon and dragged it under a table, I closed my eyes and bathed in sunlight. *How I loved the sun! I had forgotten how to enjoy the warmth of it without fear! I stood and spun around the room, laughing at the freedom I now experienced. I was free from the darkness!*

"Why do you daydream, Queen Guinevere? Come now! You cannot stay a maid forever." My ladies giggled at Broca's words, their pink lips curled with excitement. And how could we not feel excited? This was the beginning of the age of chivalry.

I lost myself in the welcome memory, for surely this was only that, and I could not help but smile back at them. I was so delighted to see them after all this time. Their joy and laughter quenched any sorrow I felt. I sensed another standing near me and could in fact see his shadow beside me. Merlin! If this is a pretense, a memory, let me stay here, Merlin!

I remembered their names now, each of them. Yes, I knew Broca, Lady of the Southern Falls immediately. And there was Dayna, the daughter of the Red Knight, the only girl in the kingdom who had hair redder than mine; and my other three companions, all sisters, Edgarda, Everleigh and Evelyn. These three were Sir Kay's daughters, considered plain by some cruel gossips at court, but truer ladies a queen could never ask for. They led me to the adjoining chambers, and I said goodbye to my kitten and promised to come back for him soon. It was a simple room, really, with nothing much in the way of furniture except a massive bed, two chairs and a small table. In the corner stood a long, polished bronze mirror, which was quite a prize to own. I immediately shuffled to the table laden with fresh fruits and bread, poured myself a cup of wine and listened to my friends chatter away. The wine burned my tongue; I was not accustomed to drinking it in those days. At my father's court, one drank honey mead or perhaps lemon water.

I had forgotten the taste of grapes, Merlin.

I drank the whole cup. Yes, I remembered this day, and here I was in it again. I could smell fresh herbs, which had been lovingly bundled and hung around my bed for luck. I took in the scent of lavender lotion, which Broca lavishly rubbed on my hands and arms. My ladies showered my cheeks with kisses and hung love amulets around my neck before they began braiding my hair, weaving small white flowers in some of the braids. The hair matters were interrupted only by the sounds of music coming up from the hall below. The men were celebrating with Arthur as he waited for his bride to ready herself. I swatted my ladies' hands away.

"That is enough. Not too many braids."

Evelyn whispered in my ear, "Now, remember what Broca's mother told you. And you must promise to tell us everything, Guinevere. I mean, my queen. Tell us everything, remember?"

I laughingly pushed them out of the room without making such a promise. "Go now, silly ones. I will see you soon." Their sweet presence distracted me and made me even more anxious. I would be married to the High King of Britain, a beautiful, brave young man whom I vowed to not only honor with my body but also protect at all times. *And Excalibur. I would have to protect the sword! I was married to it too.*

What were my ladies thinking? I would never share with them what passed between my husband and me during our time alone. Unlike my sillier friends, I knew how important it was to keep secrets in marriage, even at my young age. *Yes, I had been young once. How long ago that was!*

And I had no reason to suspect that Arthur would lack confidence in this arena. I strongly desired my husband, but that did not matter so much in our society. Who knew if you would marry an old man or a young man? Young women did as we were told, but it was not that way with Arthur and me. He always asked me what I thought; in fact, he asked me to marry him before he ever spoke to my father. Arthur said he knew Leodegrance would never refuse him, but he did not want to force me into marriage if I loved another. That day I told him the honest truth, that I loved no one except him.

I waited in my room for an hour or more. The wooden chair offered no comfort, as it had no padding at all, so I eventually moved to the bed and sat on the edge of it. I regretted not bringing the kitten with me and hoped that the curious animal did not manage to get lost in my absence. The sun was setting, and I could hear well-wishers singing beneath my tower; my own ladies had joined in the celebration with the gathering crowds. I could hear their voices in the songs, and I prayed they kept their wits about them during this time of frivolity. They were now ladies of the High Queen, and their lives were not merely their own but were in service to the Pendragon and all of Britain. And then the heavy door opened.

Oh yes, I remember this moment. I had expected Arthur, but Morgan had come instead.

"Guinevere, we are to be sisters. True sisters now! Let me serve you, sister. Arthur will come to you soon." She turned back the thick covers of our marriage bed and then stoked the fire. "It will be cold this evening. You will need a warm fire. Or maybe you won't." Morgan's mischievous smile made me blush. "What are all these?" She put the poker aside and stalked toward me. "Love charms? I do not think you need them." Before I knew it, she had removed my gifts, and I allowed her to do so. I would reclaim them later, I promised myself. Morgan insisted that I change into an elegant nightgown that she presented to me; the garment was much finer than the one I now wore. Impressed, I allowed her to help me change and took a minute to admire the fit in the mirror. It was as if the thing had been made for me.

"A picture of beauty, my queen and sister." She kissed my cheek and smiled back at me in the mirror. "I hope that I am as lucky one day. I have found the one I want to marry. He is in the court now."

"Tell me, Morgan, who is he? King Lot is too old for you, I think."

"No, not Lot." With a dreamy expression she confessed that her own suitor, or so she hoped, had arrived at Camelot just this hour, a man named Lancelot. He had greatly impressed the young king and even Igraine, which was not an easy thing to achieve. Morgan rambled on about Lancelot's strength in battle, his handsome face, the beautiful Lake Lands and his elusive mother, Vivian, the Lady of the Lake, from whose hands Excalibur had been given to the Pendragons. It seemed an odd thing that she would share such personal information with me, as she had never been one to do so before, but I was happy for her despite my surprise at her openness. Nervously, I chewed on my fingernails. She playfully swatted my hands as the door opened again.

Igraine called to Morgan, "Daughter, come. It is time to leave. The king approaches." Igraine, tall and lovely, smiled briefly at me before the two of them disappeared. I had hoped she would speak to me and wish me well, but she did not. Instead of joy, her lovely face was the picture of sadness.

And then in came another, but not the one I expected. It should have been Arthur who stepped into the room. Yes, I remembered this. It should be Arthur!

Merlin...

"Why are you here?" I asked him, not really wanting to know the answer. This wasn't just a memory, this was *my* memory—a sweet memory that I did not want to end. I peeked around him, hoping that Arthur would emerge from behind Merlin's broad shoulders, that I would see his handsome face again, see his cheerful smile and hear him speak my name. But he did not emerge from the gray hallway.

Only Merlin remained, and even the sounds of rejoicing dimmed and the edges of the room blurred. "Let me stay here," I pleaded with Merlin, whose expression I could not read. My pulse raced, my skin warmed. I could hear footsteps and laughter in the hallway as the bridegroom's party escorted Arthur to our chambers. My senses were alive, infused with excitement and gladness, and I knew that this one moment, this one day had been the pinnacle of my long life. My happiest moment. The one I dreamed of the most, longed for the most.

I now lay again in darkness. The keep of Camelot had vanished, and Merlin was my only companion. He sat beside me on the floor, not touching me but too near for my liking.

"No," I screamed, my voice rising with grief. "No!" I did not care who heard me. I did not care about anything except returning to that sweet moment. And for the first time in nearly seven hundred years, I cried. *How is this possible?* As I wept, my skin warmed slightly and I felt something I had not felt in a long time. Something beyond sadness and the dreariness of a life of endless darkness. "You are cruel, Merlin," I whispered as I lay with my face hidden from him.

"Many say that I am. I am sorry to hear that you are one of them."

I sat up and pushed the hair back from my face. I wiped away the dampness and heaved another sob. Strangely relieved, I said, "I have become what you said, Merlin. I am the White Death."

"You are, Guinevere. But you need not remain so."

His words shook me to the core. Rising from the ground, I probed his mind again, but it remained impenetrable. Too bad he could so easily plunder mine. I had underestimated him.

"How can that be?"

"Because you are married to a Greater Power."

"I do not understand."

"You kissed the sword—and it kissed you back. Arthur inherited Excalibur, but you...it *chose* you, Guinevere." I gasped to hear him say such a thing. "Why do you think you were able to hide Excalibur away from Morgan all these years? It trusts you. It sleeps, waiting for you to return and claim it."

"But Excalibur belongs to Arthur!"

"Yes, it does, and you must return it to the king's hands. As Morgan's curse weakens, she becomes more desperate. She hopes to claim Excalibur because possessing it will renew her strength."

"Why has she become so weak, Merlin? She says we will die. Is that true?"

His dark eyes shone with purpose, and his skin nearly glowed in the moonlight. "If we can keep Excalibur out of her hands, the curse will thin enough to be pierced. This will happen soon, Guinevere. However, if we fail, if she possesses Excalibur, she will be unstoppable; she will come at Arthur—and you—with new strength."

I was on my feet now. "As I told Morgan, the days of swords and kings and queens are over!"

"You think so? Why then have you searched for Arthur all these years?"

I had no answer except one. "Because I love him. I never stopped loving him."

"Then let that be enough. This man, this Arthur, is the true Arthur, Guinevere! Whether he wears a crown again or not, whether he wields Excalibur again or not, he needs you. He needs us both. And there are other forces, powers I do not yet understand, that will soon come against us. The time of kings and queens may be over, but the lust for power and the absolute corruption of it never ends. This realm, this time must be protected."

"Morgan says..."

"Do not say her name again," he warned me as he turned his head toward the doorway.

"She says Arthur will die, that this is his last life. Is this true?"

"I do not know, and I doubt that she does either. But your curse, the shee-blood curse," he said as he smiled at me now, "oh, that is on death's door. It is thin now. Hold on just a little longer, my queen. Together we will break it."

I traveled to the door and peeked out. I heard nothing and no one nearby. This would be the time to leave. "Follow me. It is not far from here."

Perhaps it was the loneliness that propelled me to take him to the sword. Did I trust the Merlin of Britain? No, never. But despite my wariness, I felt something I had not felt in a long time.

A very long time.

Hope. It came in on invisible wings and lifted my empty soul into places where I had dared not journey in many lifetimes.

Yes, I thought as I flew around a corner with Merlin's hand in mine, I felt hope.

Chapter Fourteen—Guinevere

Mossy ruins were all that remained of Saint Albans. The building's arched stone doorways had collapsed and the heavy oak doors had rotted away centuries ago. No walls stood; it was as if Saint Albans had never been, as if no songs had ever echoed through its sanctuary. Even the elegant stained-glass windows had vanished. If I did not know what it had been, I would not believe the ruin to be anything much. Most of the stones had been hauled away or were buried under the weight of the encroaching forest. A few corners of the walls remained, sprayed with vulgar graffiti. What an ill end for such a holy place.

Yet for all this decay and destruction, the sword remained unmolested, untouched. I could feel it humming beneath my feet, as if it summoned me, whispered to me, called my name. *Guinevere! Release me!*

Merlin's words returned unbidden to my ears: "Excalibur chose you."

"No, you belong to Arthur!" I murmured in the darkness, forgetting for a moment that there was another beside me. I instantly regretted speaking, and I felt Merlin watching me. Ready to retrieve Excalibur, I stepped out from behind the massive tree and then his hand was on mine. It was strange to feel the touch of another, enough of a surprise to make me pause at the edge of the tree line.

"Look, there."

We were not the first to arrive. How had I missed these mortals? A trio of young people walked the grounds cussing and chatting with one another. Were they searching for something? The tallest, the one called Billy, took a deep drag from a fat cigarette and let out a whoop. He passed the cigarette to his shorter friend, Rat, who wasted no time inhaling the intoxicating smoke. Of the three, his heart beat the strongest. If I had to choose one for my own needs, he would be the one. I could not say why. Something about the scent of him appealed to me. The third member of this ridiculous trio would be of no use to me, for I had no stomach for taking another child's life. The girl, Marley, was pregnant and had no idea which of these two prizes was the father.

"I can get rid of them," I said impatiently.

"No," Merlin cautioned as he peered at them from behind the tree. "We wait."

The three chattered back and forth for another few minutes as they stomped around the property; I grew tired of watching them. Everything about them bored me. I said as much to my companion, who replied, "If we chase them away, we will not know why they are here. Their presence here tonight cannot be a coincidence." I thought he must be wrong. The graffiti and litter attested to the fact that this once-holy place had become nothing more than a gathering place for the dregs of society. This group did not have the brain power to mastermind stealing Britain's most revered and desired artifact. I had all but written them off until the one called Rat said the word that grabbed my attention.

...sword...

Merlin leaned closer, and we scrutinized their every move. Despite my excellent sight and hearing, the surrounding forest dulled my senses. Without waiting for Merlin's approval, I bolted to the first pile of rubble. Hunching down, I peered over the stones and waited. My heart raced, and the blood hunger rose within me. Predatory behavior always excited me. Could I deny my nature?

"Where is it, Billy? You said you knew how to get in. I'm freezing my cods off out here."

"Girls don't have cods, idiot, and it's not going to be any warmer underground."

"Call me that again and I'll make you eat your teeth." Marley shoved Billy, and he drunkenly mocked her for her efforts. Once he stopped laughing, he tried to kiss her, but the girl wasn't having any of it. "I'm here for the money—nothing else. Now let's get this over with or I'm going home."

"Go home then, crybaby. We don't need your help. Nobody here believes you're psychic anyway, Mar."

"I am too! You know I am, Billy—you bastard! Even *she* says I am! She says I have the gift!"

In the chaos of the two squabbling and the third obviously searching for the entrance of the catacombs below the ancient church, Merlin scrambled up beside me unnoticed by the mortals. The two lovers continued their intense debate until Rat called them.

"Hey! Will you two shut it? I think I found it! This way! I knew it was here but just couldn't remember which corner. It's this one." Using the heel of his boot, Rat kicked at the grass and uncovered the hidden iron ring. Billy joined him, and Marley raced after him awkwardly in her high-heeled ankle boots. The three of them worked furiously to uncover the opening, but I could not let that happen.

Excalibur knew they were there. It knew and was resisting them, whether they knew it or not. I knew it because I heard the sword. I could hear it speak; it did not speak with words, but it spoke to my soul.

I am here...I am close...I watch... I closed my eyes and thought these things. Merlin looked at me strangely; had he heard me speaking to Excalibur?

"Watch this," I said with a grin on my face. "I will soon get rid of them."

"Guinevere, wait. It is better to hide and wait." He touched my hand again, but I pulled away this time.

"That is not my way. Besides, the sword is calling me. I am a vampire now, Merlin. I am the Undead Queen; I do not need your help for this." I showed him my fangs and closed my eyes to focus on my transformation. I would show myself to these humans, in all my glory. That should send them fleeing in another direction. I was frightening to mortals—I was the Bringer of Death. My fanged teeth, bloodless skin and unholy dark eyes would frighten them to their souls. I would make sure of that. I had no intention of killing any of them, unless they refused to leave. And then all bets were off.

I stood, and an unearthly wind began to blow my hair around my face. This was part of my vampire working; I could appear as an ordinary human. I could show myself to be a picture of absolute terror if I so desired, or I could look irresistibly beautiful. Tonight, Billy, Rat and Marley would see no beauty in me, only horror.

As I walked toward them, they did not yet notice me, but they soon would. I let out a scream that would curdle the blood of the bravest of knights. That got their attention. Levitating off the ground a few feet, I hovered and stared at them. I willed my skin to appear even paler, and so it did. I reached for them with outstretched hands, and the three of them simultaneously screamed. My hair, nearly black now, flew around me like snakes and I screamed again.

"It's a damn ghost! Get out of the way!"

"That's not a ghost," Marley corrected Billy. "That's something else!"

I bared my teeth at her and licked my lips with my overly long tongue. She screamed at the sight, abandoning her amateur attempts at guessing who or what I was. All she wanted to do was get away; her hand protectively clutched her stomach. I looked over at Rat and could see the kid had pulled open the hatchway that would lead down into the catacombs. He watched me with fearful eyes but did not stop. Billy was long gone; he called back at Rat, who ignored him.

Yes, this was a brave one—or a foolish one.

Suddenly, without even thinking, the sound of the sword humming beneath me, I charged at Rat and took him to the ground. My teeth were at his throat before I knew what happened.

But then I stopped drinking his blood. Something was wrong.

The young man was screaming, out of his mind with fear and feeling pain like he'd never felt before. I wanted to drink him, all of him, but something was amiss. As his blood dripped down my chin, I stared into his frightened eyes. The dark pupils were dilated with fear, and he was begging me for his life. Then the strangest thing happened to me. I lost my appetite. I stood up and stepped back from his writhing body on wobbly legs. In just a few seconds, I had taken quite a bit of his blood, and I wondered whether he would live or die. And then Merlin was there. He squatted down beside Rat and hushed him gently. And then he snapped his neck as if he were killing a chicken and not a full-grown man.

"I could not kill him," I said as I wiped the blood off my face. My dress was bloody too. I would need some new clothing soon. "I cannot understand that. Nothing like that has ever happened to me." I couldn't stop staring at Rat's corpse. *Am I feeling regret?*

"You could not kill him because he is one of yours, Undead Queen. He is of your bloodline, Guinevere."

"You lie!" I accused him. "That is not possible."

"How is it not? Alwen lived, Undead Queen. Alwen lived and married and had many children. Her offspring had many offspring and so on and so forth. It is the nature of things."

"How do you know this about my daughter?"

"Because I married her. Come now, we must retrieve Excalibur and then you must rest." The druid disappeared down the hole, and I flew after him. This wasn't over, but for the moment I had to think about Excalibur. I could hear it more clearly now. It was about a hundred feet in front of me, hidden under the blue stone where Alwen and I placed it the night she was stolen from me.

"Did you steal my daughter from me, Merlin? Is that why you hid from me all these years? Did your guilt keep you away?" I shouted into the darkness and searched for him. I did not have to wait long. There he was, glowing about ten feet ahead of me.

He turned to face me. "I rescued Alwen. Morgan captured her and was selling her to the highest bidder. I claimed her, and Morgan had to release her to me. We were happy together, Undead Queen."

"Stop calling me that!" I said as I swatted away a patch of spider webs. "Where is my daughter, enchanter?" Merlin hated to be called that—he felt it beneath him, which was precisely why I used it now.

"She lived only once, Guinevere. She was not twice-born, no matter how much I wish she had been. I would have found her again and loved her still. I would have kept her safe." I gasped to hear him speak so freely about loving my only daughter, my sweet, innocent Alwen.

And then I heard the sword speak loudly, "*...Guin...light...Arthur...*"

"Stop talking," I said to Merlin. "Listen! Do you hear it?"

"Guin...light...Arthur...broken..." I whispered the words I heard the sword speak.

Merlin asked, "Is the sword speaking to you now?"

"Yes," I said, feeling like I was in a trance. "It calls me. It wants to tell me a secret."

"What does it say, Queen Guinevere?"

"*Guin...light...Arthur...broken...*I do not understand what it says."

"Take the sword, Guinevere! Take it now! Morgan will be here soon, I fear."

"I cannot take it yet. It is speaking. It is warning me. It wants me to know..."

Aggravated, Merlin reached for the blade himself. But as soon as his hand touched it, a spark erupted from the steel and he hit the floor as if he were dead. Anxious to make contact with Excalibur, I slid it out of the decrepit blanket where I had hidden it all those years ago and gasped at the sight of the blade. *Still lovely and perfect and dangerous! The Sword of Britain! My sword!*

"No, Guinevere! It is Arthur's sword! You must return it to him! You must!"

I held the sword up and felt it throbbing in my hands; it was as if Excalibur and I had never been apart. How could I have not missed this feeling? Power surged through the blade, up my arm and all through my body. Yes, this was a strong blade wrapped in strong magic.

Magic strong enough to break this curse for good. I held it up for a moment and then without thinking began spinning about with the blade upraised and my face turned up to the ceiling. The sword and I were one! I could see what it saw, feel what it felt.

Excalibur remembered. It remembered its breaking, the breaking of what could not be broken. It remembered, and it had not forgiven Arthur. The sword had not been stolen, as some had supposed. It had wanted to go with Morgan. She had wooed the force in the blade, offered it a place of honor and much blood and glory. Morgan promised that she would never break Excalibur, that she was the true Pendragon, but the sword remembered me and found its way back to me.

"Guinevere, my queen, we must leave this place. Arthur, I can see him. He is in danger. We must go take him the sword or all will be lost!"

"Yes, to Arthur," I said dreamily as we left the catacombs with the sword.

Yes, we will bring it to Arthur and see what Excalibur thinks about that.

Chapter Fifteen—Luke Ryan

"Guinevere," I whispered aloud. I heard a female voice humming near me, and someone shuffled around me. The inky blackness made it impossible to discern who or what drew near. My mouth felt dry, as if I had worked all day in the mine without breaking for a drink of water. "Who's there?" I strained to see in the darkness. *Where am I?* A crackling of stones fell to the ground a few feet away, and then I knew exactly where I was—the Cavanaugh Mine. I tried to stand up, but my head was reeling. My hand flew to the source of the pain, and I cringed at my own touch. I had a sizeable lump at the back of my head. *Am I bleeding?* I felt sick to my stomach. *This can't be good.*

A match strike changed everything. A woman's face appeared above mine. Her dark hair hid her face as she waved her hand over the flame of the large white candle she held. And then she lit another candle and then another and set them in the recesses of the cave walls. *How many candles does she have? This isn't safe!* Who was she? I'd seen her before but couldn't place her. The lump on my head throbbed. *I should know her!*

"Guinevere!" I couldn't help but call that name.

"Yes! Call her, by all means, my king. Call Guinevere, but you should know a few things about your wife. She is quite changed, not as you left her. She is demon-kind now, brother. She betrayed you, betrayed us both, and you know the price for betraying a Pendragon—but I punished her. Guinevere was always your weakness, Arthur."

Arthur! Yes, I am Arthur. I could not make sense of her words...what could she mean? My head ached intensely, but my heart was beating like a gazelle's.

"Morgan. You are Morgan." She grinned at my realization but came no closer. Footsteps echoed down the hall, and a man cleared the narrow entrance of the small room. I didn't remember this room, but this was definitely the Cavanaugh. He ducked to avoid hitting his head, and by his height and swagger I knew who he was—McAllister. *Rat bastard!* I sat up and discovered my left hand was shackled to the wall. A spike had been driven deep into the stone, and a makeshift cuff trapped my wrist.

"You didn't die after all? I thought I killed you back there."

"It would take more than you to kill me, McAllister. What the hell are you doing here? Better yet, why am I here?"

"Lucy tells me you stole something valuable from her and she wants it back. So..." He grabbed me by the back of the head and snatched it up. "Tell her what she wants to know."

"When did you become my sister's dog, McAllister?" My ex-boss hit me in the gut with his clenched right fist, and I gagged at the pain. I swore at him and promised to tear him a new one. He didn't seem too concerned. *Man, I'm in bad shape. I've got to keep it together*. Where the hell was Buddy? Any other time I wouldn't be able to shake the old man, but now he was nowhere to be found.

"Come here," Morgan commanded McAllister. They kissed savagely, and he openly groped her. Who or what had brought these two together? The sight of my ex-boss fondling my sister shocked me, but I had an even bigger question.

"Why am I here? What do you want, Morgan?"

"Excellent question, my king." She pushed McAllister away and walked toward me; I was her complete focus now. She tugged at the cuff, reminding me that trying to free myself would be futile. "Do you wonder why I cuffed only one hand? I will tell you why—because I love seeing you struggle! And with one hand free, you'll fight to the death if needed, which is what I want you to do. You will fight and lose, Arthur. So be patient...this will all be over soon."

"What do you want?" I demanded as I tried to get to my feet. I leaned against the wall, but the cuff wouldn't budge.

"None of this should surprise you. Why do you deny me, brother? Am I not a Pendragon too? You know what I want—I want what is mine. But no matter, Guinevere is bringing it to me."

"I don't think so, Morgan. She would die before she let that happen."

"She is already dead," she said as she slapped me hard across the side of my face. I swung at her with my free hand, but she laughed as she ducked away from me easily. She moved faster than I could have predicted. It was an inhuman movement. Her words chilled me to the core.

"What are you, Morgan? What have you become? What have you done to Guinevere?"

"Oh, I did nothing, really. She made it so easy. Imagine how unqueenly, taking one's own life, but it did her no good; she could not escape payment for her crimes."

The hair on my arms rose at her words. "What crimes do you speak of? I am the one who refused to hand over Excalibur to you. I am the one who killed your son on the battlefield. Whatever justice you demand, you do wrong by asking Guinevere to pay the blood-price."

Morgan let out a scream of anguish when I mentioned the death of Mordred. She began to breathe heavily and, to my amazement, grew a foot taller right in front of my eyes. She screamed again, and her fingers extended; they looked like something out of a horror flick. Morgan was becoming...something, and the sight of her beastly transformation scared the hell out of me. I looked at McAllister's face; he was also terrified and stepping back toward the entrance. Morgan's lovely face contorted, her already large eyes changed, and her face took on a wolfish look. Holy hell! Was she a werewolf? Immediately I began tugging at the cuff. I leaned against the wall, using my feet to push off, hoping that would free me. And then Morgan began to talk.

But I did not understand the words. They were ancient and deadly and focused on me. I was about to die. I had been on many battlefields in my first life and through many dangers in my current life, but none had been as menacing as Morgan was now.

Before Morgan could complete her transformation, Guinevere raced into the room, her beautiful face twisted with anger, her eyes glittering with determination as she sailed into the chamber. Her hands flew around McAllister's neck, and she took him to the ground with a growl. I watched in horror as she pounced on him with the ferocity of a beast. McAllister made a gurgling sound but soon lay still on the cave floor. Another figure entered the small room—the place was getting crowded now, and I was eager to get out. I recognized the face. Merlin! He ran to my side immediately and began working on the cuff. I could not help but stare at my old friend. I clamped his shoulder with my hand. "Thank God you've come." To think, Buddy...no, Merlin had been with me all this time. As we struggled to weaken the metal cuff, Morgan charged at Guinevere, the candles flickering as she moved. Guinevere disappeared through the low doorway and reappeared with Excalibur. How were they moving so quickly? I could do nothing but stare as they circled one another, spinning and growling. Guinevere's dark red hair flew around her; she looked fierce, and all her determination was focused on Morgan. I thought perhaps she would swing the sword and make the blow, but she did not.

"Arthur!" Guinevere shouted, her voice raspy yet strong. Like an expert marksman, she flung a tiny silver knife at Morgan and pinned her hand to the cavern wall. Black blood dripped from the wound, and a scream of rage issued from my sister's throat. As if I were watching the events in slow motion, Guinevere then launched the sword at me. I thought that she would kill me, that I would die, but suddenly Excalibur rested in my hand. *As if it had a mind of its own!* I flicked my wrist instinctively and discovered that my arm was now free from its chains.

"Excalibur!" I exclaimed as the cave began to shake and rock. Morgan had freed herself from the silver knife and began to scream; the sound was unholy and chilled me to my bones.

"Give it to me!" She slashed at Guinevere with the silver blade, and my wife fell back for a moment. Her face bled, and her white teeth glistened in the candlelight. What was wrong with her teeth?

"Guinevere!" I screamed in horror.

Merlin yelled at me. "Run!" he warned me as he reached for Morgan and climbed on her back. "You have to leave now!"

The mine shook again, small rocks began to rain down on us, and suddenly arms were around me and I felt myself flying. I clutched the sword, ready to do battle with Morgan. Merlin had fallen off her back, and she charged at him with the silver blade. Guinevere carried me effortlessly from the cave as it began to collapse. Her strange perfume wrapped around me and brought me comfort in the chaos.

"Merlin!" I yelled, but there was nothing I could do. Guinevere and I flew into the bright light that leaked into the cave portal. Then she screamed and released me as we breached the opening. She collapsed in the dirt in a heap of agony. Her cool skin felt hot now, and her eyes were pools of dark pain. Her cries revealed her fangs again, and the sight horrified me.

"Arthur! The light!" she moaned, but there was no time to wait for her to explain. The mine exploded behind us, a shower of rocks covering the entrance.

"Merlin!" I yelled as Guinevere crawled away at record speed. She hid under Buddy's familiar van and crumpled into a ball. "Merlin!" I did not know what to do, race back to save Merlin or help Guinevere.

"Arthur! Please, help me! I am burning!" Guinevere wept.

When the ground stopped rumbling, I snatched open the van door and grabbed an emergency blanket out of the first-aid kit. My heart raced as I crawled under the van to cover her smoking body. "Guinevere," I said, but she only moaned in response. Covering her face and body, I dragged her out from under the van.

"No, Arthur..." she cried in breathless pain. "Do not look at me!"

"You need a hospital. We have to go!"

"No, no hospital. Take me to the darkness or I will die."

I deposited her in a heap on the passenger seat and drove Buddy's van like a madman to the place where my mind led me. I felt like someone was guiding me, and then I realized Guinevere was showing me the pictures in my mind.

Turn here, yes, left. Arthur, I am burning!

In twenty minutes we were driving on a narrow path through the thick woods, almost straight into a long-forgotten ruin. This had once been Cameliard, or at least a piece of it. Before I knew what was happening, Guinevere was flying into the remains of her once-proud tower, a trail of smoke behind her.

Chapter Sixteen—Arthur Pendragon

I ran behind Guinevere with Excalibur in my hand. I wept as I ran—the loss of Merlin was great, and now I was losing Guinevere. Or had I already lost her? What had happened to her? This sudden revelation, of who I was and who I'd been, was too much. I had no time to think...and I needed to think. I ran down the narrow stairs. She had to be down here. There was nowhere else for her to go.

"Guinevere! Where are you?" I clutched the sword and yelled again, "Guinevere, don't run from me. I need you. We have to go back for him. We must..."

She whispered back to me from somewhere below, "Sleep, Arthur. I must sleep. Please stay away. I cannot trust myself to be close to you now. I hunger..."

As I reached the bottom step, I waited for my eyes to adjust to the dimness. She was there, my disheveled queen, a smoking mess. Her hair covered her face, but I could see how colorless and frail she was. "What has happened to you? What can I do?"

"I must sleep, Arthur." She rolled her head toward me, and I could hardly believe I was looking on the face of my wife. How could I have ever forgotten her? Her skin was so pale, her lips paler, and her hair had darkened to a deeper red, but time hadn't changed who she was. She was still my queen, my love, my Guinevere.

I laid the sword between us and sat beside her. Should I hold her? Would she set upon me as she had McAllister? She had warned me, and I could hear the fear in her voice. Yes, she had warned me to leave her be, but I could not. I could not resist moving the strand of hair that crossed her face. As I did, her eyes flew open and she grabbed my arm. I could feel the ferocity surging again behind those wide eyes that had once been as green as emeralds and were now dark and full of pain.

"Arthur?"

"I am here, Guinevere."

"Do not look at me," she whispered breathlessly. "I do not want you to see me like this. Remember me as I was. Leave me now."

"Never! I will never leave you."

Suddenly, I could see her walking down the long aisle of the church, her ladies walking behind her. How Camelot had celebrated their new queen! How the people had loved her!

Then I saw my son, my only son, Lochlon, on the day he began to practice on the fighting field. How proud I had been. No man ever had been as proud as I was of my son. But where was he now?

Lochlon!

Guinevere squeezed my hand, and I realized that once again she was guiding me, showing me what she remembered, reminding me of the love we once shared.

Remember this, Arthur. Leave me now.

"Never," I said aloud as I closed my eyes and continued to watch the memories unfold in her mind. My daughter, Alwen! Her mother's shadow, the light of my heart! And I could see the knights gathering at our Round Table. Fantastic dreams we had shared. Hopes of a better world, of happier times before the wars with my sister drained all the brightness from our kingdom. I wept at the life, our lives. We had lived in a time of magic, in a special time, but nothing of it remained now. Nothing except Guinevere and me.

Leave me, Arthur. Remember yesterday and leave me.

No...I continued to hold her hand and enjoy her memories, for they were mine too. Memories of Guinevere and me together, making love in the woods. Hunting with Kay and his daughters. I remembered the fires of May, the sounds of laughter in the hall...and then Morgan's face hovered before me. Her mouth moved, but I could not hear her.

I never wanted to hear her again. Then the memories ended as Guinevere fell asleep.

"Guinevere, I am here. Rest now."

I watched over her for hours. I wept and clutched her cold hand until my own eyes grew heavy, and when I opened them, she was gone. I was alone with Excalibur and my dreams of yesterday.

Epilogue—Arthur Pendragon

"Roll to the left, Pint. Ten degrees."

"Got it, boss." The young man moved the joystick of the miniature tractor and grabbed a shovel full of rubble from the collapsed portal of the Cavanaugh Mine. Seeing the first heap of rock moved lifted a load off me. We were one step closer to finding Merlin.

"Keep at it. One step at a time."

I unrolled the map and reviewed it for the fifteenth time today. "Okay, Norman, let's move a few loads out to here and get started erecting those beams. We have to secure them as soon as possible. Then we're in for more."

Norman smiled at me good-naturedly. I was glad to learn that McAllister had been lying to me. The older Wheeler never had any intention of suing me. He was advising caution now, and I was not ignoring his advice. "We'll find Buddy, boss, but he wouldn't approve of losing someone else in the process."

"You're absolutely right, Norman. And I have no intention of losing you or anyone else. We do this by the book."

"You got it, boss."

Feeling worried, or maybe just needing some reassurance, I asked, "Do you think he's...I mean, the chances of him being alive...."

Norman patted my shoulder. "We'll know soon enough. It's only been a few days, and stranger things have happened. Let's get on it. Hey, Pint!" He was off to help guide Pint out of the portal.

I made more notes on the map, highlighting potential weak spots in the mine's structure. Morgan's booby trap had collapsed a small but pivotal area, just as she'd designed it to do...or as McAllister had designed it to do. If it hadn't been for Guinevere, I would be sealed inside too. But none of these guys knew about any of that, and I planned to keep it that way.

At least the Cavanaugh Mining Company was behind me. They wanted to recover McAllister and Buddy, and they had asked for my help with that. Now that the gear was here, we would work night and day to see it accomplished. Men with a purpose could do anything they set their mind to, and what greater purpose was there than rescuing a friend?

Merlin, can you hear me? It's me, Arthur. I am coming for you, Merlin. Just hold on a little while longer.

No answer came, and all I knew to do was to keep digging. Merlin was all I had left. Guinevere was gone—I got the distinct impression that she visited me in my dreams, but it was not enough. I could not remember them, only fleeting images and shadows. I wanted to see her, be with her, but she had not reappeared to me so far.

At least she had left me Excalibur. I glanced at my truck and tapped on my key to make sure the alarm was set. Maybe that wasn't the best place to leave your sword, but I couldn't bear to part with it, even for work.

And as long as the sword was near, Guinevere was too. Excalibur connected us. It was a fact, one that I could no more explain than I could explain how I had come to be alive again. I put on my hard hat and went to work. It was no crown, but I was proud to wear it. I might not have been a king anymore, but I still had a job to do and guys to lead and protect. I had to believe that everything would work out.

By whatever strange magic had brought us together again, Merlin, Guinevere and me, it could not be in vain. There had to be a reason.

There must be a Greater Purpose in all this.

For hours we shifted stones out of the mine and set braces along the way. We were getting closer now. So close that I could hear someone whispering...

Norman looked at me, and I stared back at him. "Is that a voice?" he asked.

I nodded, and we began loading our carts with rocks.

Someone was alive! Someone was talking!

Merlin, I am coming!

More from M. L. Bullock

From the *Ultimate Seven Sisters Collection*

A smile crept across my face when I turned back to look at the pale faces watching me from behind the lace curtains of the girls' dormitory. I didn't feel sorry for any of them—all of those girls hated me. They thought they were my betters because they were orphans and I was merely the accidental result of my wealthy mother's indiscretion. I couldn't understand why they felt that way. As I told Marie Bettencourt, at least my parents were alive and wealthy. Hers were dead and in the cold, cold ground. "Worm food now, I suppose." Her big dark eyes had swollen with tears, her ugly, fat face contorting as she cried. Mrs. Bedford scolded me for my remarks, but even that did not worry me.

I had a tool much more effective than Mrs. Bedford's threats of letters to the attorney who distributed my allowance or a day without a meal. Mr. Bedford would defend me—for a price. I would have to kiss his thin, dry lips and pretend that he did not peek at my décolletage a little too long. Once he even squeezed my bosom ever so quickly with his rough hands but then pretended it had been an accident. Mr. Bedford never had the courage to lift up my skirt or ask me for a "discreet favor," as my previous chaperone had called it, but I enjoyed making him stare. It had been great fun for a month or two until I saw how easily he could be manipulated.

And now my rescuer had come at last, a man, Louis Beaumont, who claimed to be my mother's brother. I had never met Olivia, my mother. Not that I could remember, anyway, and I assumed I never would.

Louis Beaumont towered above most men, as tall as an otherworldly prince. He had beautiful blond hair that I wanted to plunge my hands into. It looked like the down of a baby duckling. He had fair skin—so light it almost glowed—with pleasant features, even brows, thick lashes, a manly mouth. It was a shame he was so near a kin because I would have had no objections to whispering "Em-brasse-moi" in his ear. Although I very much doubted Uncle Louis would have indulged my fan-tasy. How I loved to kiss, and to kiss one so beauti-ful! That would be heavenly. I had never kissed a handsome man before—I kissed the ice boy once and a farmhand, but neither of them had been handsome or good at kissing.

For three days we traveled in the coach, my uncle explaining what he wanted and how I would bene-fit if I followed his instructions. According to my uncle, Cousin Calpurnia needed me, or rather, needed a companion for the season. The heiress would come out this year, and a certain level of de-corum was expected, including traveling with a suitable companion. "Who would be more suitable than her own cousin?" he asked me with the curl of a smile on his regal face. "Now, dearest Isla," he said, "I am counting on you to be a respectable girl. Leave all that happened before behind in Birming-ham—no talking of the Bedfords or anyone else from that life. All will be well now." He patted my hand gently. "We must find Calpurnia a suitable husband, one that will give her the life she's accustomed to and deserves."

Yes, indeed. Now that this Calpurnia needed a proper companion, I had been summoned. I'd never even heard of Miss Calpurnia Cottonwood until now. Where had Uncle Louis been when I ran sobbing in a crumpled dress after falling prey to the lecherous hands of General Harper, my first guardian? Where had he been when I endured the shame and pain of my stolen maidenhead? Where? Was I not Beaumont stock and worthy of rescue? Apparently not. I decided then and there to hate my cousin, no matter how rich she was. Still, I smiled, spreading the skirt of my purple dress neatly around me on the seat. "Yes, Uncle Louis."

"And who knows, ma petite Cherie, perhaps we can find you a good match too. Perhaps a military man or a wealthy merchant. Would you like that?" I gave him another smile and nod before I pretended to be distracted by something out the window. My fate would be in my own hands, that much I knew. Never would I marry. I would make my own future. Calpurnia must be a pitiful, ridiculous kind of girl if she needed my help to land a "suitable" husband with all her affluence.

About the *Ultimate Seven Sisters Collection*

When historian Carrie Jo Jardine accepted her dream job as chief historian at Seven Sisters in Mobile, Alabama, she had no idea what she would encounter. The moldering old plantation housed more than a few boxes of antebellum artifacts and forgotten oil paintings. Secrets lived there—and they demanded to be set free.

This contains the entire supernatural suspense series.

More from M. L. Bullock

From *The Ghosts of Idlewood*

I arrived at Idlewood at seven o'clock thinking I'd have plenty of time to mark the doors with taped signs before the various contractors arrived. There was no electricity, so I wasn't sure what the workmen would actually accomplish today. I'd dressed down this morning in worn blue jeans and a long-sleeved t-shirt. It just felt like that kind of day. The house smelled stale, and it was cool but not freezing. We'd enjoyed a mild February this year, but like they say, "If you don't like the weather in Mobile, just wait a few minutes."

I really hated February. It was "the month of love," and this year I wasn't feeling much like celebrating. I'd given Chip the heave-ho for good right after Christmas, and our friendship hadn't survived the breakup. I hated that because I really did like him as a person, even if he could be narrow-minded about spiritual subjects. I hadn't been seeing anyone, but I was almost ready to get back into the dating game. Almost.

I changed out the batteries in my camera before beginning to document the house. Carrie Jo liked having before, during and after shots of every room.

According to the planning sheet Carrie Jo and I developed last month, all the stage one doors were marked. On her jobs, CJ orchestrated everything: what rooms got painted first, where the computers would go, which room we would store supplies in, that sort of thing. I also put no-entry signs on rooms that weren't safe or were off-limits to curious workers. The home was mostly empty, but there were some pricy mantelpieces and other components that would fetch a fair price if you knew where to unload stolen items such as high-end antiques. Surprisingly, many people did.

I'd start the pictures on the top floor and work my way down. I peeked out the front door quickly to see if CJ was here. No sign of her yet, which wasn't like her at all. She was usually the early bird. I smiled, feeling good that Carrie Jo trusted me enough to give me the keys to this grand old place. There were three floors, although the attic space wasn't a real priority for our project. The windows would be changed, the floors and roof inspected, but not a lot of cosmetic changes were planned for up there beyond that. We'd prepare it for future storage of seasonal decorations and miscellaneous supplies. Seemed a waste to me. I liked the attic; it was roomy, like an amazing loft apartment. But it was no surprise I was drawn to it—when I was a kid, I practically lived in my tree house.

I stuffed my cell phone in my pocket and jogged up the wide staircase in the foyer. I could hear birds chirping upstairs; they probably flew in through a broken window. There were quite a few of them from the sound of it. Since I hadn't labeled any doors upstairs or in the attic, I hadn't had the opportunity to explore much up there. It felt strangely exhilarating to do so all by myself. The first flight of stairs appeared safe, but I took my time on the next two. Water damage wasn't always easy to spot, and I had no desire to fall through a weak floor. When I reached the top of the stairs to the attic, I turned the knob and was surprised to find it locked.

"What?" I twisted it again and leaned against the door this time, but it wouldn't move. I didn't see a keyhole, so that meant it wasn't locked after all. I supposed it was merely stuck, the wood probably swollen from moisture. "Rats," I said. I set my jaw and tried one last time. The third time must have been the charm because it opened freely, as if it hadn't given me a world of problems before. I nearly fell as it gave way, laughing at myself as I regained my balance quickly. I reached for my camera and flipped it to the video setting. I panned the room to record the contents. There were quite a few old trunks, boxes and even the obligatory dressmaker's dummy. It was a nerd girl historian's dream come true.

Like an amateur documentarian, I spoke to the camera: "Maiden voyage into the attic at Idlewood. Today is February 4th. This is Rachel Kowalski recording."

Rachel Kowalski recording, something whispered back. My back straightened, and the fine hairs on my arms lifted as if to alert me to the presence of someone or something unseen.

I froze and said, "Hello?" I was happy to hear my voice and my voice alone echo back to me.

Hello?

About *The Ghosts of Idlewood*

When a team of historians takes on the task of restoring the Idlewood plantation to its former glory, they discover there's more to the moldering old home than meets the eye. The long-dead Ferguson children don't seem to know they're dead. A mysterious clock, a devilish fog and the Shadow Man add to the supernatural tension that begins to build in the house. Lead historian Carrie Jo Stuart and her assistant Rachel must use their special abilities to get to the bottom of the many mysteries that the house holds.

Detra Ann and Henri get a reality check, of the supernatural kind, and Deidre Jardine finally comes face to face with the past.

More from M. L. Bullock

From *The Ghosts of Kali Oka Road*

"Sierra to base."

Sara's well-manicured nails wrapped around the black walkie-talkie. "This is base. Go ahead, Sierra."

"Five minutes. No sign of the client. K2 is even Steven. Temp is 58F."

"Great. Check back in five. Radio silence, please."

"All right."

She tapped the antenna of the walkie-talkie to her chin. "I hope she remembers to take pictures. Did she take her camera?" she asked Midas. It was the first time she'd spoken to him this afternoon.

"Yes, but it wouldn't hurt to have a backup. You have yours?"

Sara cocked an eyebrow at him. "Are you kidding? I'm no rookie." She cast a stinging look of disdain in my direction and strolled back to her car in her stylish brown boots and began searching her back seat, presumably for her camera.

"Am I missing something?" I couldn't help but ask. The uncomfortable feeling kept rising. I'd had enough weirdness for one day.

Nobody answered me. Midas glared after Sara, but it was Peter who broke the silence.

"Cassidy, have you always been interested in the supernatural? Seems like we all have our own stories to tell. All of us have either seen something or lost someone. They say the loss of a loved one in a tragic way makes you more sensitive to the spirit world. I think that might be true."

"You're an ass, Pete. You're joking about her sister? She doesn't know she's lost her." I could see Midas' muscles ripple under his shirt. He wore a navy blue sweater, the thin, fitted kind that had three buttons at the top.

"I'm sorry, Cassidy. I swear to you I'm not a heartless beast."

"How could you not know?" Sara scolded him. "She told us about her the other night."

"I had my headphones on half the time, cueing up video and photographs. Shoot. I'm really sorry, Cassie."

That was the last straw. I was about to tell him how I really felt about his "joke." I took a deep breath and said, "My name is Cassidy, and..."

The walkie-talkie squawked, and I heard Sierra's voice, "Hey! Y'all need to get in here, now!"

Immediately everyone began running toward the narrow pathway. Midas snatched the walkie. "Sierra! What's up?"

"Someone's out here—stalking us."

“Can you see who it is? Is it Ranger?”

“Definitely not! Footsteps are too fast for someone so sick.” Her whisper sent a shiver down my spine. “I’m taking pictures...should we keep pushing in toward the house?”

“Yes, keep going. We’re double-timing your way. Stay on the path, Sierra. Don’t get lost. Follow your GPS. It should lead you right to it.”

“Okay.”

“Midas! Let’s flank whoever this is!” Pete said, his anger rising.

Midas looked at me as if to say, “Are you going to be all right?”

Sara said, “Go and help Sierra. Cassidy and I will follow.”

Immediately Midas took off to the left and Peter to the right. They flanked the narrow road and scurried through the woods to see if they could detect the intruder.

Sara handed me her audio recorder. “Hold this! I’m grabbing some photos. We’re going to run, Cassidy. I hope you can keep up.”

“Sure, I used to run marathons.” I didn’t want to seem like a wimp. Now didn’t seem like the time to tell her that I hadn’t trained in over six months. “But why are we running? Are they in danger, do you think? Maybe it’s just a homeless person.”

"The element of surprise! Hit record and come on! Get your ass in gear, girl!"

I pressed the record button, gritted my teeth and took off after her. We ran down the leaf-littered path; the afternoon sunlight was casting lean shadows in a few spots now. We'd be out of sun soon. Then we'd be running through the woods in the dark. Was it supposed to be this cold out here?

I wish I held the temperature thingy instead, but I didn't.

"You feel that, Cassidy? The cold?" She bounded over a log in front of me, and I followed her. "Not unusual for the woods, but this is more than that," she said breathlessly. "I think it might mean we've got supernatural activity out here."

"You think?" I asked sincerely.

She paused her running. Her pretty cheeks were pink and healthy-looking. She'd worn her long hair in a ponytail today, and she wore blue jeans that fit her perfectly.

"Yeah, I do. I think it's time you get your feet wet, rookie. Use the audio recorder. Ask a few questions."

"Um, what? What kind of questions?"

"Ask a question like, 'Are there any spirits around me that want to talk?'"

I repeated what she said. I spun around slowly and looked around the forest, but there wasn't a sound.

Not even bird sounds or a squirrel rattling through the leaves. And it didn't just sound dead; it felt dead.

About *The Ghosts of Kali Oka Road*

The paranormal investigators at Gulf Coast Paranormal thought they knew what they were doing. Midas, Sierra, Sara, Josh and Peter had over twenty combined years of experience investigating supernatural activity on the Gulf Coast. But when they meet Cassidy, a young artist with a strange gift, they realize there's more to learn. And time is running out for Cassidy.

When Gulf Coast Paranormal begins investigating the ghosts of Kali Oka Road, they find an entity far scarier than a few ghosts. Add in the deserted Oak Grove Plantation, and you have a recipe for a night of terror.

More from M. L. Bullock

From *The Tale of Nefret*

Clapping my hands three times, I smiled, amused at the half-dozen pairs of dark eyes that watched me entranced with every word and movement I made. "And then she crept up to the rock door and clapped her hands again..." *Clap, clap, clap.* The children squealed with delight as I weaved my story. This was one of their favorites, The Story of Mahara, about an adventurous queen who constantly fought magical creatures to win back her clan's stolen treasures.

"Mahara crouched down as low as she could." I demonstrated, squatting as low as I could in the tent. "She knew that the serpent could only see her if she stood up tall, for he had very poor eyesight. If she was going to steal back the jewel, she would have to crawl her way into the den, just as the serpent opened the door. She was terrified, but the words of her mother rang in her ears: 'Please, Mahara! Bring back our treasures and restore our honor!'"

I crawled around, pretending to be Mahara. The children giggled. "Now Mahara had to be very quiet. The bones of a hundred warriors lay in the serpent's cave. One wrong move and that old snake would see her and...catch her!" I grabbed at a nearby child, who screamed in surprise. Before I could finish my tale, Pah entered our tent, a look of disgust on her face.

"What is this? Must our tent now become a playground? Out! All of you, out! Today is a special day, and we have to get ready."

The children complained loudly, "We want to hear Nefret's story! Can't we stay a little longer?"

Pah shook her head, and her long, straight hair shimmered. "Out! Now!" she scolded the spokesman for the group.

"Run along. There will be time for stories later," I promised them.

As the heavy curtain fell behind them, I gave Pah an unhappy look. She simply shook her head. "You shouldn't make promises that you may not be able to keep, Nefret. You do not know what the future holds."

"Why must you treat them so? They are only children!" I set about dressing for the day. Today we were to dress simply with an aba—a sleeveless coat and trousers. I chose green as my color, and Pah wore blue. I cinched the aba at the waist with a thick leather belt. I wore my hair in a long braid. My fingers trembled as I cinched it with a small bit of cloth.

"Well, if nothing else, you'll be queen of the children, Nefret."

About *The Tale of Nefret*

Twin daughters of an ancient Bedouin king struggle under the weight of an ominous prophecy that threatens to divide them forever. Royal sibling rivalry explodes as the young women realize that they must fight for their future and for the love of Alexio, the man they both love. *The Tale of Nefret* chronicles their lives as they travel in two different directions. One sister becomes the leader of the Meshwesh while the other travels to Egypt as an unwilling gift to Pharaoh.

More from M. L. Bullock

From *Wife of the Left Hand*

Okay, so it was official. I *had* lost my mind. I turned off the television and got up from the settee. I couldn't explain any of it, and who would believe me? Too many weird things had happened today—ever since I arrived at Sugar Hill.

Just walk away, Avery. Walk away. That had always been good advice, Vertie's advice, actually.

And I did.

I took a long hot bath, slid into some comfortable pinstriped pajamas, pulled my hair into a messy bun and climbed into my king-sized bed.

All was well. Until about midnight.

A shocking noise had me sitting up straight in the bed. It was the loudest, deepest clock I had ever heard, and it took forever for the bells to ring twelve times. After the last ring, I flopped back on my bed and pulled the covers over my head. Would I be able to go back to sleep now?

To my surprise, the clock struck once more. What kind of clock struck thirteen? Immediately my room got cold, the kind of cold that would ice you down to your bones. Wrapping the down comforter around me, I turned on the lamp beside me and huddled in the bed, waiting...for something...

I sat waiting, wishing I were brave enough and warm enough to go relight a fire in my fireplace. It was so cold I could see my breath now. Thank God I hadn't slept nude tonight. Jonah had hated when I wore pajamas to bed. *Screw him!* I willed myself to stop thinking about him. That was all in the past now. He'd made his choice, and I had made mine.

Then I heard the sound for the first time. It was soft at first, like a kitten crying pitifully. Was there a lost cat here? That would be totally possible in this big old house. As the mewing sound drew closer, I could hear much more clearly it was not a kitten but a child. A little girl crying as if her heart were broken. Sliding my feet in my fuzzy white slippers and wrapping the blanket around me tightly, I awkwardly tiptoed to the door to listen. Must be one of the housekeepers' children. Probably cold and lost. I imagined if you wanted to, you could get lost here and never be found. Now her crying mixed with whispers as if she were saying something; she was pleading as if her life depended on it. My heart broke at the sound, but I couldn't bring myself to open the door and actually take a look. Not yet. I scrambled for my iPhone and jogged back to the door to record the sounds. How else would anyone believe me? Too many unbelievable things had happened today. With my phone in one hand, the edge of my blanket in my teeth to keep it in place and my free hand on the doorknob, I readied myself to open the door. I had to see who—or what—was crying in the hallway. I tried to turn the icy cold silver-toned knob, but it wouldn't budge. It was as if someone had locked me in. Who would do such a thing? Surely not Dinah or Edith or one of the other staff?

About *Wife of the Left Hand*

Avery Dufresne had the perfect life: a rock star boyfriend, a high-profile career in the anchor chair on a national news program. Until a serious threat brings her perfect world to a shattering stop. When Avery emerges from the darkness she finds she has a new ability—a supernatural one. Avery returns to Belle Fontaine, Alabama, to claim an inheritance: an old plantation called Sugar Hill. Little does she know that the danger has just begun.

More from M. L. Bullock

From *The Mermaid's Gift*

Dauphin Island had more than its share of weirdness—a fact illustrated by tomorrow's Mullet Toss—but it was home to me. It wasn't as popular as nearby Sand Island or Frenchman Bay, and we islanders clung to our small-town identity like it was a badge of honor. Almost unanimously, islanders refused to succumb to the pressure of beach developers and big-city politicians who occasionally visited our pristine stretches of sand with dollar signs in their eyes. No matter how they sweet-talked the town elders, they left unsatisfied time and time again, with the exception of a lone tower of condominiums that stood awkwardly in the center of the island. As someone said recently at our monthly town meeting, "We don't need all that hoopla." That seemed to be the general sense of things, and although I valued what they were trying to preserve, I didn't always agree with my fellow business owners and residents. Still, I was just Nike Augustine, the girl with a weird name and a love for french fries but most notably the granddaughter of the late Jack Augustine, respected one-time mayor of Dauphin Island. What did I know? I was too young to appreciate the importance of protecting our sheltered island. Or so I had been told. So island folk such as myself made the bulk of our money during spring break and the Deep Sea Fishing Rodeo in July. It was enough to make a girl nuts.

But despite this prime example of narrow-mindedness, I fit in here. Along with all the oddities like the island clock that never worked properly, the abandoned lighthouse that everyone believed was haunted and the fake purple shark that hung outside my grandfather's souvenir shop. I reminded myself of that when the overwhelming desire to wander overtook me, as it threatened to do today and had done most days recently. I had even begun to dream of diving into the ocean and swimming as far down as I could. Pretty crazy since I feared the water, or more specifically what swam hidden in the darkness. Another Nike eccentricity. Only my grandfather understood my reluctance, but he was no longer here to tell me I wasn't crazy. My fear of water separated me from my friends, who practically lived in or on the waters of the Gulf of Mexico or the Mobile Bay most of the year.

Meandering down the aisles of the souvenir shop, I stopped occasionally to turn a glass dolphin and rearrange a few baskets of dusty shells. I halfheartedly slapped the shelves with my dust rag and glanced at the clock again and again until finally the shark-tooth-tipped hands hit five o'clock. With a bored sigh, I walked to the door, turned the sign to Closed and flicked off the neon sign that glowed: "Shipwreck Souvenirs." I'd keep longer hours when spring break began, but for now it was 9 to 5.

I walked to the storeroom to retrieve the straw broom. I had to pay homage to tradition and make a quick pass over the chipped floor. I'd had barely any traffic today, just a few landlubbers hoping to avoid the spring breakers; as many early birds had discovered, the cold Gulf waters weren't warm enough to frolic in yet. Probably fewer than a dozen people had darkened my door today, and only half of those had the courtesy to buy something. With another sigh, I remembered the annoying child who had rubbed his sticky hands all over the inflatables before announcing to the world that he had to pee. I thanked my Lucky Stars that I didn't have kids. But then again, I would need a boyfriend or husband for that, right?

Oh, yeah. I get to clean the toilets, too.

I wondered what the little miscreant had left behind for me in the tiny bathroom. No sense in griping about it. It was me or no one. I wouldn't be hiring any help anytime soon. I grabbed the broom and turned to take care of the task at hand when I heard a suspicious sound that made me pause.

Someone was near the back door, rattling through the garbage cans. I could hear the metal lid banging on the ground. Might be a cat or dog, but it might also be Dauphin Island's latest homeless resident. We had a few, but this lost soul tugged at my heartstrings. I had never seen a woman without a place to live. So far she had refused to tell me her name or speak to me at all. Perhaps she was hard of hearing too? Whatever the case, it sounded as if she weren't above digging through my trash cans. Which meant even more work for me. "Hey," I called through the door, hoping to stop her before she destroyed it.

I had remembered her today as I was eating my lunch. I saved her half of my club sandwich. I had hoped I could tempt her to talk to me, but as if she knew what I had planned, she'd made herself scarce. Until now.

I slung the door open, and the blinds crashed into the mauve-painted wall. Nobody was there, but a torn bag of trash lay on the ground. I yelled in the direction of the cans, "Hey! You don't have to tear up the garbage! I have food for you. Are you hungry?"

I might as well have been talking to the dolphins that splashed offshore. Nobody answered me. "I know you're there! I just heard you in my trash. Come out, lady. I won't hurt you." Still nobody answered. I heard a sound like a low growl coming from the side of my store.

What the heck was that?

Immediately I felt my adrenaline surge. Danger stalked close. I ran to the back wall of my shop and flattened myself against the rough wood. I heard the growl again. Was that a possum? Gator? Rabies-crazed homeless lady? I knew I shouldn't have started binge-watching *The Walking Dead* this week. There was absolutely nothing wrong with my imagination. My mind reeled with the possibilities. After a few seconds I quietly reasoned with myself. I didn't have time for this. Time to face the beast—whatever it might be.

About *The Mermaid's Gift*

Nike Augustine isn't your average girl next door. She's a spunky siren but, thanks to a memory loss, doesn't know it—yet. By day, she runs a souvenir shop on Dauphin Island off the coast of Alabama, but a chance encounter opens her eyes to the supernatural creatures that call the island home, including a mermaid, a fallen goddess and a host of other beings. When an old enemy appears and attempts to breach the Sirens Gate, Nike and her friends must take to the water to prevent the resurrection of a long-dead relative...but the cost might be too high.

To make matters worse, Nike has to choose between longtime crush, Officer Cruise Castille and Ramara, a handsome supernaturate who has proven he's willing to lose everything—including his powers—for the woman he loves.

Read more from M.L. Bullock

The Seven Sisters Series

Seven Sisters
Moonlight Falls on Seven Sisters
Shadows Stir at Seven Sisters
The Stars that Fell
The Stars We Walked Upon
The Sun Rises Over Seven Sisters

The Idlewood Series

The Ghosts of Idlewood
Dreams of Idlewood
The Whispering Saint
The Haunted Child

Return to Seven Sisters
(A Sequel Series to Seven Sisters)

The Roses of Mobile
All the Summer Roses

The Gulf Coast Paranormal Series

The Ghosts of Kali Oka Road
The Ghosts of the Crescent Theater
A Haunting at Bloodgood Row
The Legend of the Ghost Queen
A Haunting at Dixie House
The Ghost Lights of Forrest Field

The Sugar Hill Series

Wife of the Left Hand
Fire on the Ramparts
Blood by Candlelight
The Starlight Ball

Lost Camelot Series

Guinevere Forever

The Desert Queen Series

The Tale of Nefret
The Falcon Rises
The Kingdom of Nefertiti
The Song of the Bee-Eater

The Sirens Gate Series

The Mermaid's Gift
The Blood Feud
The Wrath of Minerva

Standalone books

Ghosts on a Plane

To receive updates on her latest releases, visit her website at MLBullock.com and subscribe to her mailing list.

84809847R00091

Made in the USA
Middletown, DE
21 August 2018